Rob Gauld-Galliers has had   as an architectural TV & movie prop model maker, story board and scenic artist, illustrator, set designer, character developer, art director and production designer for commercials, cinema and television. He was the art director on the television series *Thomas the Tank Engine & Friends*, (Series 1 to 10), set designer on *Tugs, Jack & the Pack,* production designer on *Here Comes Mumfie, Orsum Island & Mike DA Mustang* and designed Thomas Land at Fuji-Q Highland, Yamanashi, Japan.

Rob was a display pilot flying various WWI and WWII aircraft and a pilot on the movie *Flyboys* plus a couple of TV series.

He now lives in Cambridgeshire with his wife, and Belka, the little blue Staffie, enjoying semi-retirement to the full.

To my wife, Jane.
For her patience and encouragement.

Rob Gauld-Galliers

THEY WHO DARED

AUSTIN MACAULEY PUBLISHERS™

LONDON • CAMBRIDGE • NEW YORK • SHARJAH

A CIP catalogue record for this title is available from the British Library.

ISBN 9781398407589 (Paperback)
ISBN 9781398407602 (ePub e-book)
ISBN 9781398407596 (Audiobook)

www.austinmacauley.com

First Published 2023
Austin Macauley Publishers Ltd®
1 Canada Square
Canary Wharf
London
E14 5AA

Max

Chapter One

The early morning sun cast long shadows across the old rectory garden and gave the dew moistened leaves a glistening golden edge.

'I love the warm sunshine more than anything,' whispered Max to himself as he rubbed the sleep from his eyes.

That night he had made a cosy nest high up in a small cavity on the face of an old brick wall. It was a safe place to sleep for the night and if by some misfortune he came back this way again, he would definitely use it. The domestic dog, cat or fox was his biggest fear, but he did have a way of dealing with them. If one showed interest in him, he let out a hornet like buzzing sound. The reaction was instant, recoil, ears back, flick of the tail and off. Inquisitive squirrels were not so easy to fool, but at least they didn't see him as a juicy meal!

Meal! Yes, that's what I need, something to keep me going through the day, thought Max. He swept his dusty-fair unkempt hair away from his deep brown eyes and eyed up a blackberry bush. One juicy blackberry would supplement his nourishment pill nicely. Max's plan was to take a quarter of a pill a day and conserve the ration he had taken from base two days earlier.

Base was where Max had grown up and been trained. Grown up, that was a joke, he was fifteen years old and would never be much taller than a one and a half litre bottle of water or, roughly, thirty centimetres. Max was the product of a top secret and very restricted experiment, code named in Latin, "Omina videmus" – "we see all things". The organisation was top secret, even the director general and the government knew nothing of its existence, well not yet. The plan was to perfect and present to only the right, most qualified end user who would pay for their service handsomely. Receiving government funds for the umbrella organisation O.B.W Pharmaceutical Research which was operating in the research establishment located several miles to the southwest of Reading in Hampshire, "Project OV" was multi-layered and camouflaged deep below and within the catacombs of the establishment. This was the brainchild of one anonymous ex-MI5 top agent and involved five brilliant scientists, all emotionally unattached, supposedly dying nineteen years previously when the helicopter they were on board disappeared over the North Sea on its way to Copenhagen. The conference they were due to attend was to discuss a revolutionary range of pharmaceutical drugs. In fact, all were very much alive and paid extremely well but living under false identities, if you could call it living. No families, only the family of their labour, of which one, was little Max.

Max and the fifteen others of his age group were all miniature humanoids, physically scaled down in size.

The product of advanced "DNA" manipulation.

His group were the oldest. The younger ones were being educated and trained, just as Max had been. Trained in the art of covert operations and intelligence gathering, to see and not be seen, to listen and not be heard. Their main target, to combat international terrorism, infiltrate dubious networks and enemy cells seeking to carry out "high impact" terrorist attacks around the world and terminate them.

He could plant and defuse explosives. Go to ground, hide, listen and report or give co-ordinates on enemy cells for targeting, or even down to very simple low-grade tasks like immobilising vehicles, and playing a part in fragmenting small terrorist cells. There were many ways to create unrest while the target subjects were under extreme pressure.

They were tough, Spartan-like, miniature special operational beings, and would become fully mature and ready for active service at the age of eighteen. However, they would never grow much above their current height.

Max and his little group had enjoyed practicing their skills. In their free time, they had great fun creeping around the establishment, crawling through ducting, hiding behind the scientist's desks and listening to their technical talk or idle chit chat. They had accidentally learned through their ability to eavesdrop during one of those play practices times, their ultimate fate. On completion of their training and upon reaching eighteen years of age, they would have a small operation, a device would be planted in their bodies, miniscule and as light as a feather, the height of nanotechnology. This would be carried with them for the rest of their lives, or, until they were discovered. The device could be remotely activated and automatically explode, vaporising them and taking their finder with them, eliminating all evidence. The detonation of the minute device would cause a chromosphere within a millisecond, five times hotter than the surface of the Sun. The hot gases in violent motion would destroy all immediate evidence. There was another question on their minds. Would the establishment use them as involuntary walking bombs on contact within the enemy cell, even if not discovered by the enemy?

This was the reason Max and his fifteen-year-old colleagues were scattered in the outside world. They had successfully escaped, but into a world of danger, better that than being dispensable. Eternal vigilance was now the price of freedom. How could the establishment do that to them? He knew the reason, to cover their tracks, no bodies no proof, no love, no care and no life.

The establishment had failed their task in the mechanism and practices of total indoctrination, and now Max's group would stubbornly seek freedom.

On an overcast warm summer's morning, they exercised and chatted as normal in the outside safe area. Annexed to the research establishment and surrounded by overgrown wartime bund walls, this place was a very secure, isolated plot of land once belonging to the military and covering several acres.

As planned, they waited until the two supervisors walked over to fill in the roster sheets at the old guard house, now renamed for its commercial facade, the security building.

This usually took five to ten minutes to complete the paperwork. That time would be just enough for the group to run to the overgrown bund wall, then up and over into the wooded area on the southeast side of the complex and escape under cover of the ferns and undergrowth. If all went well, the idea was to crawl through a small culvert under the razor wired electric perimeter fence where they had hidden their scaled-down "Ghillie" suits, camouflaged clothing they used during their training. Most important were the operations bags, specially made scaled-down trekker type rucksacks full of survival equipment. They would rapidly dress, help each other put on their rucksacks then split into their known pairs. They would find it easier to evade capture in pairs.

Max had teamed up with Flea, a strong-willed girl with almond-shaped pale blue eyes, short, dark thick hair and attractive pointed features that belied the fact that she was as hard as nails. She said little and did not suffer fools gladly. He liked her, she was strong, both mentally and physically and could really look after herself if the going got tough.

Flea had reacted very badly after finding out about the self-destruct plan. Fortunately, although seriously disillusioned and hurt, her training meant she was able to keep it all bottled up within. The group could only be successful in their escape plan if the supervisors were given no clue to the disappointment and anger felt by Max and the others.

Flea

Max pushed his fingers through his hair and wondered where Flea was right now. They had become separated during an attempt to cross a wide stream. Flea knew better and insisted she would find a narrower crossing place further

13

along the bank. Max stubbornly went on trying to cross at his chosen point and against all their training, they had allowed themselves to be separated. For that Max could kick himself.

Wading across, using a spear like stick to support himself, Max reached almost halfway when suddenly he heard voices. He turned and with all the strength he could muster, fought his way back to where he had just come from. Scrambling out of the water, he threw himself under the overhanging grass and tree roots that topped the stream bank. Nervously, he watched his wake slowly disperse downstream, a dead giveaway to his location.

Moments later, two anglers walked by, or were they anglers? Peering out from his hiding place Max noticed that although they carried fishing rods and bags, the stream was just too shallow and narrow to catch anything of worth. They could be part of a covert search team, "hunters", dressed up as anglers, hikers, so as not to arouse suspicion, sent out by the establishment to track down members of the fugitive group.

The pair walked in the direction Flea had gone. She must have heard them coming along the bank, as he had done.

If they had not been chatting and kept their mouths shut, they would have spotted me halfway across, thought Max.

A chill ran down his spine. What would their fate be now? The project would be terminated and all evidence would be swept under the carpet along with him and his little group, no they were more than his group they were his little family of friends, that's what they were.

At least no raised voices downstream, no splashing about, that was a good sign.

Go Flea, go!

Max sat eating his breakfast with his legs dangling over the edge of his nest wondering how he would find Flea and the rest of the group.

While making their plans for escape and survival back at the establishment, Cork, one of the boys who had an interest in all things to do with aviation, had suggested meeting at Copham, a small airfield with grass runways for light aircraft some miles to the south he had read about in a magazine. There was always a windsock on an airfield and they would try and meet under it, suggested Cork. Not a daft idea when Cork explained it all. When they got within a mile or two of the airfield and if the weather were reasonable, they would be likely to see an aeroplane or two flying in and out. This would be their beacon. The A303 dual-carriageway road passed along its southern side, so the group should never unknowingly stray past it. Simple. *Only one small problem,* thought Max. *They would take forever to even get within a mile of the place and take just as long again covering the remaining mile.*

Anyway, time to go. There was a lot of stooped walking, running, crawling, climbing and hiding to do today.

Max threaded his way along the base of the wall letting his hand gently stroke the moss that grew thick there. Moss was a good camouflage to supplement the "Ghillie" suit, he had pulled up a clump of dry moss yesterday and stuffed it into the webbing of his rucksack. If need be, he could pull it out and use it as a sort of ill-fitting poncho to break up his silhouette. It was as light as a feather as well.

'Josh, darling, come on.'

'Yes, Mummy, coming.'

Max looked up and froze. A child wearing a blue primary school uniform holding a half-chewed apple jumped out of nowhere and scampered passed him across the garden and through a door in the house opposite the wall where Max crouched.

Max took a deep breath and regained his composure. The scientists had joked with the group once...

'If you don't behave, we'll give you all to a toddler to play with!'

To be carried around by one leg and used as a sort of floppy hammer like a well-abused action man doll, did not appeal to Max at all, in fact the thought made him shudder.

OK, young children avoid at absolutely all cost. If ever one did manage to grab him, well he would just have to bite and flail around like a wild thing and suffer the drop.

Who would believe the little one?

'Mummy, a tiny weenie boy just bit my hand.'

Imagine, growing up knowing that a tiny weenie boy actually did bite your hand and the injustice of no one believing you. All the more reason to avoid this ever happening.

Max watched the large silver Volvo pull out of the drive and down the lane in a cloud of swirling dust.

He moved through the flowerbed to the kitchen door and let himself in through a cat flap. Lowering the flap down gently behind him, he moved towards the kitchen cabinets. Opening the first revealed cans of cat and, ah... dog food.

Better watch out here.

Fortunately for Max the dog was in the back of the Volvo and would no doubt be having a frenzied sniffing session when he came back into the house. The next cabinet was more rewarding, inside stood two boxes of cereals. Max pushed over the first box and pulled the top open. He scooped out enough cereal to fill his bag.

He then went straight for the sugar bowl perched on the worktop above. Two lumps would give him enough energy for weeks.

'No take one, why spend energy carrying energy?' he muttered under his breath to himself.

Some matches, a short length of string and a handful of bits and bobs that could come in handy.

Max muttered a quick thank you and sorry under his breath as he slid out through the cat flap.

Chapter Two

The early afternoon sun cast Max's short-hard shadow onto the dusty bridle path as he stealthily crossed, ducking under the lower rust encrusted strand of an old barbed wire fence.

He parted the tall dry grass that stood just beyond and looked down into a huge meadow.

'I wonder if Flea or the others are down there,' he whispered softly to himself as he scanned the wooded hills shrouded in a summer haze that stretched from east to west.

It'd be like trying to find a needle in a haystack, no, even worse than that, a pinhead in a barn full of hay. His heart sank.

To walk around the edge of the meadow would take more than the rest of the day. But it would be madness to attempt to go straight across. Although all his instincts screamed at him to take the first option, he decided to go for the direct crossing. There were no grazing animals and no sign of humans. Max gathered a large bunch of tall dry grass that stood higher than him. This was to be used as camouflage. He tucked it through the straps and webbing of his rucksack and tied his belt around the rest. With the "Ghillie" jacket and dry grass he resembled a badly assembled scarecrow, but it was effective. At a few metres to the unsuspecting eye, he would look just like a tuft of grass.

Max straightened his back and set off on the long open trek. The grass was not long enough to give good cover but long enough to make the going tough. After covering about ten yards, Max knew this open crossing would take the rest of the day to complete.

He frequently scanned the sky for hawks or other large birds of prey. If spotted, he would freeze absolutely still and hold his stick spear-like and at the ready, until they flew off. This was a procedure they adopted even in the grounds of the establishment. It was always a serious threat when they crossed open areas. The scientists had discovered that most creatures seemed to have a natural visual profile of their various prey. This instinct went back tens of thousands of years. The profile of a miniature person did not seem to fit into their natural prey identification program. Any creature that came at you fast, grabbed you and had to make up its mind in an instant, was a danger. By the time it decided that you smelt, felt, screamed and struggled differently to its usual prey, you would be dropped. In the fall the damage would be done.

Max heard a low drone high above in the sky. Looking up he saw a biplane; it was very high and heading south. Was it on its way to Cork's airfield? If it was, he had miles and miles to travel. He wondered if Cork realised how big Hampshire was. He must have had some sort of clue, surely?

By early evening the sun had turned milky and eventually disappeared behind a high veil of grey cloud. The sky towards the northwest looked dark and threatening, the temperature dropped. Rain was coming and Max still had a very long walk ahead of him to reach the wood on the southern edge of the meadow. He quickened his pace knowing that being caught out in the open in torrential rain and being so small would cause him to lose his bearings. He would stagger around in the mud, drenched through, cold and weary he knew he would not see the night through.

Half an hour passed and Max could now see the distant hills grey and fuzzy in rain. He tucked his stick through the straps of his rucksack and broke into a run. The weight of the rucksack and long grass slowed him down, his rucksack was packed with his survival kit and could not be discarded.

To Max's horror, lightning flashed within the grey mass, then a low rumble reached his ears.

Through his panting breath he muttered, 'Hail stones.'

Thunderclouds often brought hail with them. A typical lump of hail was as large as a tennis ball to Max, being hit by one would be catastrophic!

Heavy rain was now falling on the far side of the meadow and moving towards him rapidly. A cold damp wind blew the long grass around. This was it! Max was totally exhausted his run was now a zig-zagging stagger. A heavy drop of rain punched his shoulder then a crashing blow from behind pitched him forward with such ferocity it rendered him unconscious.

The rush of cold air made Max come around with a start. It seemed he was out for a long time but was in fact only a matter of a second or two. He was looking down at the surface of the meadow whizzing past just a few feet beneath him in a green blur. A surge of panic and fear struck him.

His left arm was painfully clamped and his body was suspended by the straps of his rucksack...

'Rucksack.'

He reached around with his free arm and grabbed his stick. Pulling it through the straps of the sack, he jabbed it upward into the chest of a huge hawk. The hawk reacted instantly by swerving causing Max to nearly drop the stick. With all the strength left in him, he pushed the stick up into the chest once again, shouting at the top of his voice, 'LET GO, YOU…'

Max hit the ground with a tremendous jarring thud and slid through the whipping grass on his back at speed. Just above him the hawk was gaining height dodging and swerving from left to right. A green curtain rushed in to view wiping the underbelly of the hawk from his sight.

Max lay on his back in complete silence, hurting and in a state of shock looking up at the canopy of leaves above him. He realised that this was the line of trees, the edge of the meadow.

He slowly moved his legs and arms a little.

Good. No broken bones, just a few cuts and bruises and a slight headache from that impact with the ground.

A clap of thunder bought him to his senses. He sat up. The rucksack lay several metres away, no stick though. *Ah good, there it was.* Collecting the precious bag and stick, Max hobbled into the shelter of the trees just as heavy hail fell loudly slapping the leaves above him.

Max threw his rucksack down, painfully pulled off his "Ghillie" jacket and flopped down into the mouth of a big moss-covered hollow branch fallen from an old oak tree. Curling up into a snug ball and scooping dry leaves up around him, he let the erratic heavy drumming of hail falling onto his log from the tree canopy above woo him into a sound sleep.

Max stayed in this spot throughout the next day recovering from his ordeal.

A little fire in the mouth of the log camp kept the damp chill away. Munching on a flake of sugared cereal and looking through the shimmer of heat from the fire, he watched the damp mist from the heavy rain hanging low like a big grey ghost laying on its side over his meadow.

'That was a lesson learnt,' he muttered to himself, 'If I had taken the long way around, I would most probably be near the same spot or beyond and feeling a lot less beaten up. That was close, very close.'

Max thought back to the "survival in the wild" training they had been given by an ex-SAS soldier who worked for the establishment named Mr Joel.

He had taught them everything he knew and a lot of stuff he didn't know, like being attacked by a bird of prey when you're as small as a rabbit!

Mr Joel's words rang in Max's ears.

'Right, you lot. Always take time to look up. It could be a drone or an eagle. Got it?'

A thin smile spread across Max's lips.

I bet that little episode would have impressed old Joely.

The early morning sun found Max walking along a well rutted farm track on his march south. The track headed southeast so at some point Max knew he would have to turn onto a right heading. He could see a footpath sign ahead and decided to take it.

"Footpath to Oakley" the sign read. No other clue other than some vague village name. Max would give anything for a map, but a map would be far too big for him to carry. If the group had more time to prepare, they could have possibly acquired a map from one of the supervisor's lockers, or a desk draw maybe, then scribbled down various routes on small bits of paper and hidden them until the big day. *No use punishing myself now,* thought Max as he whacked the seeded top of a dandelion with his stick. The seeds flew up into the air above him and parachuted gently away with the light breeze. Max smiled, straightened his back and marched on.

Something caught Max's ear, a faint sound. Instinctively he scurried off the footpath for cover. The thick thorn hedge on either side of the path prevented him from getting through it in time. So, wedging himself between two roots, he pulled out his moss blanket and hid under it. He peered out and waited.

'If there's a dog coming, I've had it. Is there still time to…'

Too late. Someway down the path and coming his way were a couple riding mountain bikes. Max breathed a sigh of relief, at least no dog … *Oh no.*

A little way behind the pair scampered a terrier, weaving left and right with its nose to the ground like a demented metal detector. Whoosh… the pair cycled past at speed followed by the weaving dog. There was a loud scraping sound as the dog skidded to a halt on the loose gravel, his face already turning in the direction of Max before he had even stopped. Max wished the earth would swallow him up, he braced himself and peered out from under the moss at the rapidly approaching black shiny nose. The first dib of the nose, then followed by rapid sniffing which blew dust up all over Max. He knew that he had to act on the second dib before the dog could get too excited at its find of the day. The hornet buzz sound trick followed by a sharp jab of his stick sent the terrier into an even more crazed frenzy. Now it was barking and growling, its ears bolt upright, head tilting inquisitively left and right, it spun around a few times sending gravel flying in all directions, then…

'Rob… ROB.'

A distant yell and the terrier turned his head if though to confirm, it was he who was being called! …

'ROB, COME ON BOY.'

He gave one last look in Max's direction, popped out his tongue and bolted up the path to catch up with his owners.

Max realised he had not taken one breath of air during that whole episode. He gulped down air into his lungs, pulled down the moss, brushed the dust out of his hair, threw his head back and laughed.

'Dogs … they are totally insane!'

Chapter Three

The Oakley Village Church tower peered above the trees. Crows flapped around it making such a din, crows always seemed to be intolerant of each other.

Max lips creased into a wry smile.

'If there was another life, I definitely wouldn't like to come back as a crow, much rather be a dog, a small terrier maybe.'

Max moved over to the shadowed side of the path. He would have to be extra vigilant now and try to skirt around the outside of the village. The awful din the crows made did not help his listening out for danger at all.

Max squeezed through the bars of an iron gate into a sun dappled garden. Two squirrels hopped about busying themselves with early acorns while a wood pigeon stood not far away, staring at him with its head turned side on through one big bulging eye.

'Hey, what's the matter with you? Never seen a tiny human before?'

'Oh… maybe you have.'

Taking care not to disturb a grounded drowsy wasp nearly the size of his foot, Max moved along the base of the garden wall then crossed over an open paved area to what looked like a good plant cover.

'Strange plants… tomatoes.'

Huge red tomatoes nearly twice the size of his head hung all around him. Max was not a great fan of tomatoes, but he was thirsty and really fancied a drink.

He reached up and cut a little hole into the bottom of the ripest one. Pressing his hands firmly on either side, he squeezed and gulped down the refreshing juice. As he drank his eyes wandered around. He liked the look of tomatoes, hanging like big red party balloons. It was a cheerful place, all red and green.

On each birthday, back at the establishment when they were younger, the supervisors would pin up red, silver and gold balloons as the birthdays came around, it was cool until one burst and nearly concussed them all! The birthdays all fell in the same month, November. Max frowned.

Weird! We most probably all popped out of a test tube in that month!

Max spluttered, choked, and pushed the tomato aside. On the third plant along was another ripe slightly withered tomato, in its base was a neat hole just like the one he had cut. Max looked down at the base of the plant. No footprints just dry hard soil. *Could it have been an insect, a caterpillar, or one of the others? Maybe Flea?*

As Max threaded his way from garden to garden, he searched for tracks or any clue for the possibility that one of the others had passed that way. *The chances were not that far removed,* thought Max as most well-worn footpaths would eventually lead to a village or town, and if this one was leading him, it may have led the others too. In an attempt to avoid the village, they too would take a similar course around the perimeter gardens. Max felt excited at the prospect of spotting, creeping up, and jumping out on one of his lost friends.

The hunt was on! Max would be far more vigilant, and would scan left and right as he went on his way now, he had another element to his travels. This would help him keep going.

Running water?

Max was curious, why could he hear running water? Crawling through a small, jagged hole in an old ivy-covered trellis garden fence, he found himself kneeling at the edge of a large pond, more like a lake to Max.

The sound of burbling water came from a stream that ran through a low arch in the back wall, cascaded down a rocky gully and dropped into the pond. He popped his head up to see what he could see. Fortunately, the cottage stood some distance away sitting on a large plot of extremely high grass and brambles, it looked derelict with its windows boarded up with old floorboards nailed haphazardly in place.

Perfect! I will camp here for the night.

Usually, Max preferred quieter places to rest not because of the noise disturbance, it was just the fact that the running water covered any sound of impending danger. However, he could see that this place had not been visited by anyone for a long time.

Max set up a small temporary shelter near the arch using broken bits of fence tied together with lengths of string he acquired at the cat flap house.

If he had to, he could scramble through the arch and make his escape.

The shelter opening overlooked the pond.

This would be a pleasant place to camp. Time to light a little fire, eat, then I'll put my feet up.

After having a modest meal of a small tomato slice on toasted cereal supplemented with his quarter cut of nourishment pill, Max reclined on a soft bed of dry leaves, placed his hands behind his head and admired the view. Reflected in the surface of the large pond was the azure blue summer evening sky with salmon pink clouds dancing in the rippled water. Max felt himself drifting off to sleep and didn't resist.

The next morning Max woke to the sound of birds singing the dawn chorus. Even when he had camped in the woodland, he had never heard such an effort by all the different local birds. Noticeable by their absence from the bird calls were the crows.

All laying in, revving up and saving their breath for a bad-tempered argumentative day ahead, mused Max.

Something caught Max's eye. He instinctively ducked down. Over on the other side of the pond and a little way along, was, what looked like a small fishing rod sticking out of the long grass, it poked out at about his waist height and looked to be held by someone his own height.

So many questions filled his mind.

Could that be one of the others? Why had they not seen him first? Could it be Flea?

Max considered throwing a small pebble into the water near the rod to get a reaction but decided to put on his 'Ghillie' jacket, pull up the hood and creep around the back to get a better look. This could be a trap.

A few minutes later Max was crawling through the long grass behind the angler. Who was it?

He was crouching on all fours his heart beating fast, so fast and loud he thought it would give his position away.

Whoever it was kept perfectly still as if frozen, maybe asleep. It was a "he" … what the?

IT'S A TRAP.

Max threw himself down in fear, for sitting holding the rod appeared to be an old plump bearded man with a dirty, crumpled red hat and green coat.

Max's anxiety quickly faded as he noticed that this strange effigy had been sitting there for a long time. Matted grass roots covered his lower torso and although once colourful, he was now speckled with lichen and faded by the sun.

Max gasped, rolled onto his back, covered his eyes with the back of his hand and convulsed into fits of laughter. He had read in depth about the huge statues on Easter Island and the Mayan stone effigies hidden deep in the jungles of Columbia in a National Geographic magazine back at the establishment library. The fear that these great stone characters would have put into the ancient civilisations who worshiped them. Never in a million years would he had thought that a simple little garden gnome would have scared him senseless!

'Ah you complete wally.' He chuckled.

Max rolled over and studied the gnome. Whoever sculpted this ridiculous little old man had given him a rather pleasant face, he had a big smile and the hint of once rosy cheeks that made Max smile.

He noticed embossed lettering on his lower back, clearing the matted grass away it read, "Fisherman Gnome Number Six".

Max sat down beside the gnome and placed his arm over its shoulder.

'Caught much lately?'

The water in the pond was not too cold, in fact it was exactly right for a wash.

Hey, why not a swim? thought Max as he settled onto a partly submerged rock and lowered his legs into the water.

Within a minute Max was effortlessly and silently swimming across the width of the pond. He reached the edge and turned towards the waterfall. Under the cold falling water he ducked his head and washed his hair vigorously.

Max sat by the waterfall and let the warm sun dry him. For fun he launched a little raft on the pond made from the roof of his shelter. He watched the raft glide the length of the pond and dock itself between lily pads, and then it jerked a little, and again. Nibbling the edge of the raft was a large fish. Max was amazed at its beauty; its bright orange colouring made more vivid by the dark olive depths of the pond.

What sort of fish was this? Max and his group had never seen or heard of a "goldfish" before. Their knowledge of wildlife was all about survival, danger and food, therefore the harmless goldfish played no part in his education.

Wonder what it tastes like? thought Max as the goldfish flicked its tail making a loud splosh and disappeared into the depths of the pond as though it could read his mind.

Max glanced over to the Gnome.

'I'd like to see you try and catch that one Fisherman Gnome Number Six. Right, time to get going.'

Max spun around and took a step, his foot came to rest on a large moss-covered pebble which rolled and threw him off balance, he staggered and fell right into the toothed leaves of a stinging nettle.

The leaves swept across his neck, stomach and chest and stung badly as he yelled out in shock and staggered back brushing his exposed skin with his hands in vain. Max realised he had to act fast. For a boy of his age, the sting of a nettle would mean a painful rash, an aggravation, but for Max at his size a cocktail of formic acid and histamine would certainly have life threatening effects. There was no immediate painful discomfort just a sharp tingling sensation, but Max knew that within a minute or two he could be rolling on the ground delirious.

Max felt horribly alone and helpless.

'I must not panic,' he told himself over and over again.

Suddenly his tutor's words on survival came rushing back into his head. He desperately scanned the nearby greenery for a dock plant. Rubbing a dock leaf against the affected area of his body would help ease the rash. No luck. What else?

Max was fast becoming overwhelmed by a paralysing tingling sensation, he needed to act fast. *Cool water will ease the pain. The pond.*

Sliding down into the pond Max felt instant relief. Drawing in huge gulps of air Max knew he would soon be losing consciousness. By now the poison was beginning to circulate around his body, this was going to be a killer in the deep water of the pond. He tried to hold onto an overhanging clump of grass and climb out, but he had no sensation in his hands and could not grip with them, he slipped and found himself floating, becoming paralysed and unable to think properly.

Max was looking up at the sky, now a blurred blue haze, the fuzzy out of focus shape of a butterfly with its skipping flight crossed the blue and was gone.

Max attempted a futile cry for help… but not a sound passed his lips… closing in from the edges of vision, everything was becoming dark…

Max was aware that someone was holding and pressing his hand, playing with his fingers. This gentle nurse, a mother he had not known was there every time he drifted in and out of consciousness.

Unable to turn his head and open his eyes he lay for hours, or was it days and nights? Pangs of thirst gave a nagging discomfort.

I must have water. Max slowly opened his eyes. The blurred blue haze was back, the sky? The distant chorus of crows squabbling.

'What a beautiful sound. I'm alive!' he whispered to himself through dry lips… alive.

Another little squeeze of the hand!

Realisation. Who? *Is … is that you, Flea?*

Max turned his head. He was lying on his back afloat on his small raft with just his feet and hands in the water.

Somehow, he must have managed to struggle onto it, but he had no recollection of doing so.

Around one side of the raft, pond reeds had given him some sort of shade from the sun and maybe predators.

There was his nurse and comforter, the large goldfish gave another squeeze to his hand with her big trout like lips and as if knowing he had regained consciousness, she sank backwards into the olive-green depths of the pond. Max smiled.

'Thank you, friend.'

Cupping his hand, Max took a palm full of pond water and raised it to his mouth. Strength came to him with every sip. Raising his head, he looked down at his arms and chest, both were swollen and lumpy but there was little pain or discomfort until he raised himself onto one elbow. Now his skin seemed tight and blistered. Taking several more hand full of water he let them flow over his neck, chest and arms. This helped a little.

Max slid carefully from the raft into the water and shakily made his way around the reeds to the side of the pond.

Even though it felt as if he had been in a long sleep of unknown duration, Max still felt completely exhausted and needed to rest up for a day or two, enough at least to recover before setting off again.

By late afternoon he had slowly built a nest of spongy soft dry moss under a large overhanging fern and settled down with his stick, food ration and plenty of water within easy reach.

That night a slight breeze made the fern sway above him creating a pleasant swishing sound. Pulling his moss coat up under his chin and snuggling up, he slipped into a fitful shallow sleep, a sleep that had him dreaming of all sorts of things, mostly anxious or nightmarish. The one dream that would etch into his memory though, was about Flea.

In this dream, it's daytime, he's making his way along the edge of a meadow and looking up, spots her standing on a small ridge some distance away with her hand shading her eyes scanning the horizon. She has not seen him below and no matter how hard he tries to get her attention, he cannot move to run, wave his arms or shout her name. He stands there helplessly frozen like a statue and watches her turn and jog out of site into a deep dark forest.

It was two days later that Max felt fit enough to move on. He walked slowly and with extra care. Physically and mentally, he was not fully recovered, in fact, had never known himself to be so low in spirit. It was a mixture of feelings that caused this depression, the loneliness and realisation for the first time that he may never meet with the others. Was this mission impossible he pondered.

A long hard trudge to an eventual lonely death, not fighting for survival against a wild beast or the elements but simply through giving up.

Chapter Four

A cock pheasant exploded from the undergrowth flapping madly and squawking as it climbed for height, just clearing a hedgerow before it flew up into the cloudless afternoon sky.

Max shaken, picked himself up and realised how vulnerable he was. That could have been a fox he had nearly walked into hidden in the long grass.

Max's thoughts were abruptly ended, for not more than a few metres away came the sound of voices, just on the other side of the hedgerow he heard several people talking.

'I like those, but they take a lot of watering,' an elderly lady said.

A male voice replied, 'Well let us think about it and come back tomorrow because the centre's closing now, dear.'

All the people slowly shuffled off and the place became eerily silent.

Max waited for a while and then crawled under the hedge. It was more out of curiosity to see what lay beyond that led him that way.

Coloured roses stood in regimental rows, then flowers and shrubs, hundreds of them, all different shapes and colours.

Max spotted a tag hanging from a rose and being careful not to scratch himself on the thorns he reached up and read.

"Garston's Garden Centre – Welford…"

Good. This confirmed he was travelling in the right direction.

Long straight gravel paths ran between the flower beds which kept Max on the dry soil borders because gravel was such a noisy give-away. Max kept away from the distant main shop building just in case they had CCTV security cameras.

As the evening arrived and he still had a few hours of daylight left, Max planned to make a short cut through the garden centre and find a place to rest for the night within the relative safety of its boundary.

This was a weird and wonderful place for Max.

Avenues of huge glazed plant pots followed by rows of concrete squirrels, owls, hedgehogs and oversized snails, a cross between sculpture and well-preserved fossils.

Max came across an area designated for bird boxes and rabbit hutches; this would be a good place to settle down for the night. Max looked left and right to ensure the coast was clear, to his amazement standing on a low wooden bench several metres away to his right stood or sat a group of plump smiley little men in funny red pointed hats. Effigies in all various poses, one with a spade, another holding a mug and one at the end of the row holding a fishing rod exactly the same as Gnome Number Six he had found in the pond garden.

Max climbed up to take a closer look and discovered, that they were all numbered and labelled, "Digging Gnome", "Tankard Gnome" etc, but the one with the fishing rod was called "Angling Gnome" and sure enough on his back was number six!

They were all priced. Max felt a little foolish thinking back to his experience in the pond garden.

'Best keep that story to myself if I ever find the others.' he chuckled.

A garden water sprinkler suddenly burst into life, followed by another and then another. Max hobbled away looking for shelter, the last thing he wanted was to have to go to sleep soaked to the skin. He made his way to the rabbit hutches, bird boxes and kennels that had caught his eye earlier and he slumped into the nearest dog kennel. Sitting down, he pulled his legs up and wrapped his arms around them resting his chin on his knees as he looked out at the sprinkler shower.

The most vivid rainbow danced over the tabled plants and rivulets of water busily trickled along the ground taking fallen leaves and the odd sweet wrapper with them. Max had the feeling this was not going to stop for a while. He lay back on the timber floor, scrunched the moss poncho into a bundle and stuffed it under his head. He closed his eyes, listened to the water falling on the felt roof and soon fell fast asleep.

Max woke and sat up with a start, there was something rooting around outside. Pulling the moss bundle up to his eyes and reaching for his stick he stealthily moved closer to the door of the kennel. The sprinklers had stopped, there was no sound now other than the odd water droplet falling from a leaf onto the gravel path. The dim turquoise light on the horizon behind the silhouetted trees gave away the hour, around 10 p.m. There was not enough light and just a sliver of a crescent moon to help him see what was out there. Max peered around the kennel door being careful not to make the slightest sound. Almost immediately came the crunch of paws on gravel, followed by the rustling of leaves and silence. Max froze and felt around the timber wall to see if there was a door.

'Kennels don't have back doors, you idiot,' he muttered under his breath, 'Would it be a guard dog or fox? How long before it picked up his scent?'

A fox would not be as big of a problem than a large guard dog. A fox would scoot off after the first yell and hefty whack on the nose with his stick, but a dog would keep him cornered until his master came or worst, savage him. Max was in no fit state for gladiatorial combat with a guard dog. At least he was surrounded by three sturdy timber walls and would just have the open kennel door to defend. Thinking back on his decision on the relative safety and protection of the garden centres boundary, it was all now looking like an awfully bad idea.

A couple of minutes passed with no sound at all. Max relaxed his grip on the stick and contemplated moving away from the garden centre and finding elsewhere to bed down for the rest of the night. He would give it about ten minutes and then venture outside.

Max crept around the side of the kennel being careful not to step onto the gravel and aimed to go back the way he had come earlier. As he passed along the rear of a line of large shack like rabbit hutches his instincts told him he was not alone.

EEEEIK! CRASH! A large beast... a juvenile fox ran at full speed down the ramp and out of the largest hutch, skidded on the wet grass, bounced off the neighbouring hutch with a loud bang and ran at full speed towards him. Before Max could even raise his stick in defence the fox had sent him spinning to the ground, showering him with gravel as it tore away down the path and into the darkness. Max lay for a moment confused and feeling somewhat lucky. It had all happened in a split second but even in that low light, Max had glimpsed the wide-open terrified eyes of the fox.

'It can't have been me; the fox didn't even see me; I was just in his way.'

Then up in the raised sleeping compartment of the hutch at the top of the ramp came another shrill screech followed by a loud thrashing. Without hesitation, Max picked himself up and ran as fast as he could to the open hutch door, pushing it shut with a crash before whatever it was could attack him.

Max took several steps back and saw with luck the top wooden latch had fallen into place and firmly locked the door. He jumped forward and pulled across the bolt on the base of the door to make double sure.

Max gasped for air. He had not taken a decent breath since leaving the dog kennel.

Now the garden centre staff could deal with the beast in the morning, and he would be well away from here.

He was curious to see what sort of creature had scared that fox away and made such a terrifying wild noise, a badger, stoat or owl maybe?

Picking up his stick he rattled the end of it across the galvanised wire cage that covered the run to see if he could get the creature to peer out of the sleeping compartment. Max felt safe now that the door was firmly locked. He tried again. There was movement at the far end, a shuffle, he could just make out in the darkness a shape moving stealthily across the door at the top of the ramp. It wasn't a big creature at all, in fact it was upright and smaller, a skinny thing, an owl, yes it was an... no... it's...

Cupping his hands around his mouth, Max called in a quivering whisper,

'Who is it? Hello, Project OV… project OV, who is it?'

There was a moment's silence,

'It's Flea, who's that?'

'wha… FLEA! It's Max, it's Max.'

Max dropped to his knees and grasped the wire cage.

'You, Flea, you?'

Flea sprinted down the ramp, grabbed the cage making it rattle loudly and squinting to see in the darkness she gasped,

'Max, it can't, be you? Oh my! Am I pleased to see you? God, have you got measles?'

'NO! I had a very bad encounter with stinging nettles.'

Max took her fingers in his hand and squeezed them. He could see her white teeth in the darkness as she smiled at him.

'Tell me you didn't make that awful wild screech up there, Flea? I thought it was some kind of savage wild animal!'

Flea pulled her fingers back, 'Well, you're hardly a domesticated creature yourself, Max.'

Max smiled.

'No certainly, when it comes to scaring off creatures that see you as a tasty midnight snack.'

'Right, before you become a tasty morning snack out there, help me to get out of this thing.'

They both stepped back a few paces and looked up at the cage door.

'OK, I'll climb up the cage to release the latch Flea, hang on.'

Max untied his rucksack, threw it down and started to climb.

'Are you OK?' Flea asked.

'No, I'm still finding it difficult to bend my arms and legs after the blisters from the nettles, it's not Everest though.'

'Come down. I'll go up. I'm sure I can push the latch up from the inside.'

Flea reached up, grabbed the wire and started her ascent passing Max with ease.

'Be careful that wire is really sharp on the hands,' Max whispered as Flea hesitated, looked at her right hand and rubbed it on her hip.

Eventually she reached the top of the door, placed her hand under the latch and pushed up. The latch held fast. Letting out a grunt she tried again with more effort.

'It's not budging, Max, it's completely jammed. I can only get my hand through the wire, maybe you could give it a better push from your side.'

Max gritted his teeth and climbed as fast as he could to the latch.

'Hang on, I'll see if I can punch it up from the underside,' whispered Max as he clenched his right fist and gave an almighty uppercut to the base of the latch.

The whole cage rattled loudly. Flea glared at Max and held a finger to her lips.

'Shhhh… do you want to wake the…'

'The WHAT?' barked Max, shaking his hand in pain, 'The PLANTS?'

Max felt embarrassed about his little outburst.

'Sorry, Flea. Look, maybe the only way is to find some string or wire, tie it around the latch and pull it from the roof of the cage.'

By the time Max had climbed down, Flea was already on the ground, rooting around the inside of the hutch pushing here and there, desperately looking in the hope of finding a couple of staples missing or a week area in the construction of the cage. The reality was that the rabbit hutch was too well made.

Max jogged from one plant area to the other not even attempting to avoid the noisy gravel path. He scanned as best he could in the darkness up and down looking for anything that would come in useful.

Ah, he spotted it. Tied around a rather drab creeper type plant and holding it upright against a bamboo cane was a length of green string. Max stepped up onto the terracotta pot and began to untie the string, pulling this way and that, threading one length that seemed to have no end through a loop. If he had had a small blade or sharp piece of tin with him to cut the string he could have been back at the hutch by now.

Eventually the string fell away from the bamboo cane tied plant. Max leapt off the pot and ran, trailing the string behind him, leaving the creeper to slowly slump over and fall across the path like a bizarre drunken triffid.

Flea was squatting on the wooden ramp trying to pull up one of the wooden grip slats to use as a lever on the door when Max returned trailing the string.

'Great, you found some string, well done. Now get me out of here before I start to feel at home and my ears begin to grow.'

Max looked bewildered.

'Turn into a rabbit!'

Flea placed her two hands upright on top of her head, one slightly bent like a couple of rabbit ears, tilted her head and pulled her lower lip under her upper front teeth.

Max burst into a fit of laughter.

'Ooh wow, that really hurt, Flea, I haven't laughed like that in a while.'

'Please, Max, keep the noise DOWN.'

Max once again scaled the door, but this time looped the string around the latch, threw the rest of it up onto the roof and pulled himself up and over rolling onto the rough felt roof covering.

He stood with both hands clutching the string and leant back. Nothing, no jerk of the latch flicking up. Max tried again, this time with a lot more effort, tugging and changing angles but without success.

'It's totally jammed Flea; it just won't budge at all.'

Max placed the string around his waist in an abseil fashion and leapt back, ending up in an awkward heap on the roof.

'Nope, it's no good, I'll have to try and get into the shop Flea. There could be pruning shears or cutters of some sort in there and I could cut through the wire.'

Flea nervously placed her hands behind her head and watched Max drop the string to the ground and climb down.

As if choreographed they both looked towards the east. Sure, enough there was a faint band of turquoise light.

'Max, please hurry, it is going to be dawn in an hour or so.'

Max knew he didn't have the time to creep around the edges and keep off the gravel paths. He would have to take his chances with the CCTV security cameras. In no time at all he reached one of the shop doors. Max knew it would be locked but he didn't even try to push the door open and instead made his way to an area by the outside wall that had ducting running through into a large green house extension. There was just enough of a gap for him to squeeze between the ducting and wall into the shop.

Inside the vast unlit shop, Max drew a breath and crossed from aisle to aisle looking for something he could cut the wire with.

There down one of the aisles on a long line of shelves next to an office door was a huge array of small garden hand tools.

Max scanned back and forth, up and down, there, just to the right of the office door, hanging on peg board hooks was a selection of pruning shears. *Great.*

Climbing up onto the lower shelves Max hoisted himself from one hook to the other. He reached a set of basic pruning shears. The larger expensive shears looked far too heavy for him to manage. Holding onto the peg board and pushing the shears along the hook he managed to dislodge the end one and it fell tumbling to the lower shelf and cartwheeled across the grey linoleum floor.

Max looked down to check his footing for the descent then suddenly the fluorescent lighting at the front of the shop flickered on.

Max swung behind a hanging selection of garden gloves and peered out. To his horror, like a wave of light the fluorescents flickered on down all the aisles. It was blinding, he had been groping around all night in the dark and now this was brighter than daylight.

A tuneless whistle and the sound of footsteps came from the till area of the shop and they seemed to be approaching him.

A thin bald man sauntered down the aisle towards him clanking a large set of keys, stopped at the pruning shears lying on the floor and stooped to pick them up. Letting out a grunt he thrust them back onto the hook. Max flinched as the man's large hand brushed the garden gloves that hid him and almost made him lose his grip.

The man then pulled out a key from the bunch and opened the office door.

Max would have to be stealthy now, any noise and that man would hear without a doubt.

Letting himself down carefully Max decided that it would be better for Flea to stay put in the hutch until the next evening. He would have to come back as soon as the shop closed to get those shears but poor Flea, it would be like an oven inside that hutch under the midday sun.

The office door was open and Max had to wait until the man turned before he could make a move, just in case he saw him in his peripheral vision.

'Blimey.'

The man sat back in his chair, took off and wiped his glasses, replaced them and leant forward again.

'What the…'

To his horror, Max realised the man was looking at the CCTV playback.

The man pulled out the draw in his desk and started rummaging through it.

'Aaah, yes!' he exclaimed holding up what looked like a business card and slamming the draw closed, picked up the telephone and dialled.

'Hello, hello… didn't think there would be anyone there this early in the morning. I was going to leave a message. Right, it's Mr Trevor at "Garston's Garden Centre, Welford." One of your chaps visited me a few weeks back and offered a hefty reward if I spotted a small creature on our CCTV. What you called a very rare and dangerous little beast that escaped from a research centre. Is the little beast you're looking for something like a monkey? Small I mean, like a, yes, like a squirrel monkey with no tail?'

Taping the edge of the business card on the desk, Mr Trevor listened intently then straightened up.

'Ooh! You'd better come along and have a look at this then mate… don't worry, I won't say a word to anyone, not a soul… hang on, it's not going to attack my customers or staff, is it? Ah… OK it's very shy… won't attack unless cornered or threatened.

'Yep, that's it come straight to my office when you get here. Hope it's what you're looking for. The videos not got good definition mind, because it was dark, but the little critter looks like nothing I've ever seen out on my walks with Daisy. Daisy… ah, she's my little Jack Russell, she would have torn it apart I reckon if she'd been here… heh heh.'

As he said that, he sat back and gestured towards the window allowing Max to quickly tip toe past the door and run as fast as he could back to Flea.

Max told himself repeatedly under his breath, 'We have to get away, we have to go now.'

He scrambled through the gap around the ducting and back out into the golden light of dawn.

Max knew that the person on the other end of the phone must have been a hunter. Probably part of the covert search team from the research establishment who had previously approached individuals like those in a position to check the CCTV footage first, offering them large rewards in case of sightings. Most of the companies like garden centres or builder's yards around the research establishment fitted with CCTV cameras must have been approached, and the garden centre caretaker had hit jackpot.

Now it was light outside so Max scrambled on all fours when crossing the gravel paths, hoping that if seen on the CCTV he would be dismissed as a cat or some other four-legged animal but he knew it was really all too late for such a precaution.

Max reached Flea's hutch to find her hiding behind the ramp.

'It's no good Flea. The caretaker arrived and I had to hide. We must get you out right now. I heard him call the research

49

establishment and tell them he'd seen one of us on the CCTV. It seems like they have got some sort of network going with all those that have CCTV around their premises.

'Those monsters know exactly how we operate and where we are likely to go, and you can bet their going to arrive within the hour.'

Flea leaped towards Max, pushed and pulled desperately at the cage.

'Don't, don't panic Flea.'

Max realised it was hopeless. There wasn't even the possibility to dig under the hutch frame as the wire cage covered the floor of the hutch.

'Behind you Max, run, someone's coming!' screeched Flea as she scampered up the ramp and dived into the raised sleeping compartment of the hutch.

Max crouched, grabbed his rucksack, stick and ran, throwing himself under the nearest shrub.

Two men in green overalls walked briskly towards them.

Max trembled, and slowly pushed his face down into the dry leaves.

No, this can't be them so soon.

The elder of the two pulled out a sheet of paper from his top pocket and pointing to Flea's hutch and said in a gruff voice,

'It's this one, Phil, Large Bunny Shack TS702.'

The two men lifted the hutch between them with lots of puffing and panting and staggered down the path with it towards an open gate.

50

'I'm glad you've got the heavy end lad puffed the elder of the two as they stopped to re-adjust their handhold.

Their demeanour was not at all like that of the team hunting them down, that was for sure.

Max picked himself up and followed, scampering from one lot of cover to the other, keeping out of sight as best he could.

As Max reached the gate, the two men slid the hutch onto the tailgate of a large white van with Garston Garden Centre emblazoned down its side in large green letters.

A wave of panic swept over Max.

As the two men turned their backs to push the hutch into the back of the van and closed the tailgate he ran out of cover and made straight for a parked car alongside the van, skidding beneath it on his backside.

The two men climbed into the cab and the engine burst into life, humming like a huge electric toothbrush.

Max rolled out, leapt up and scampered to the rear of the van. There, between the bumper and the back axle hung a spare wheel. The gears of the van crunched and the huge mass above him slowly reversed. Max threw his rucksack over his shoulder, leapt up and clung onto the bracket holding the spare wheel as it passed over him.

Max clung on tight as the van turned out of the gate and accelerated up the road. The tarmac road surface became a grey blur speeding past below making Max feel nauseous. Closing his eyes helped, and laying his face on the dirty cold metal allowed him a better grip. The speeding up, slowing and cornering of the van was bad enough but the tyres bumping over potholes nearly shook Max from his perch.

Above him locked in the hutch, Max imagined Flea scared witless, not knowing he was actually with her she would obviously feel very vulnerable and alone. What was going to greet them at the van's destination? Was this journey going to last much longer? At least the longer the journey the greater distance between them and the garden centre.

Chapter Five

A large black Mercedes 4x4 swung through the gates of the garden centre and drove straight up to the farm shop entrance ignoring all one-way signs and parking bays. Two smartly dressed men wearing three-quarter length Barbour coats climbed out of the vehicle and strode into the shop.

'HELLO,' roared the smaller aggressive looking one of the two.

A small elderly woman munching on a cereal bar and clutching a mug of tea peered up from behind a till at the checkout.

'Were looking for Mr Trevor?'

She nodded her head in the direction of a weathered face peering over a display unit.

'Ah, good morning gentlemen. Gosh, that was quick! It's OK Pauline, they're from the local council and have come to see me about the proposed new extension.'

Mr Trevor turned away and gave an exaggerated wink at the two men.

'Right, walk this way. Ooh sorry, didn't catch your names?'

The elder man gestured to his colleague.

'Mr Bill and I'm Mr Davis, how do you do?'

Mr. Trevor thrust his hand out to shake hands but as there was no response awkwardly re-directed it to adjust his watch strap.

'Would you like a tea or coffee?'

'No, err, no thanks, we haven't got a lot of time, Mr Trevor.'

Turning to make sure they were out of Pauline's ear shot Mr Davis murmured, 'I know you must be busy so we'd like to have a look at this CCTV sequence and hear as much as you know or have seen, then maybe search the garden area, you know, see if we can find tracks etc. and then get out of your hair, um way.'

Mr Trevor subconsciously ran his hand over his bald head and pressed the re-wind button on the CCTV recorder. He watched the digits count down rapidly and jabbed the stop button.

As the video re-played, the two stood behind Mr Trevor, his hand eagerly poised hovering over the monitor screen ready to point out the mystery creature.

'There it is, there look, hang on I'll rewind, now watch the path there just past the big urn, see not clear but that ain't no cat, eh?'

Both men looked at each other behind Mr. Trevor's back and nodded.

'I think there's another sequence here.'

'Ah! Here we are, look at the path just there,' Mr Trevor said pointing to the top right corner of the screen.

'It's not as sharp as the other one but, heh heh, look at the thing go, look, look, its running like one of those lizards I've seen on documentaries running on its back legs.'

'Where does that path lead to Mr Trevor?'

'Call me Ted, Mr Trevor seems a bit too…'

Ted was cut short by Mr Bill as he snapped, 'Right, where was he heading there in that last sequence?'

'Er … going that way would lead to the bird and pet areas.'

'OK, Mr Bill, Mr Tre… Ted let's have a wander over and check those areas out.' Mr Davis grunted and pulling Mr Bill's arm walked briskly out of the office door.

The trio moved swiftly out of the shop and down the path to the garden area.

Ted turned to the two men.

'So, come on spill the beans, what is this little critter then? Is it a new species discovered in the deepest Amazon or an alien creature from a distant planet like that film "Alien"? Heh, heh. I bet the press would love this if they got hold of it pay an absolute bomb I shouldn't wonder, eh?'

Mr Bill raised his finger to his lips and gestured behind Ted's back and turned with a stern look nodding to Mr Davis.

'Right, this is about where the little critter was caught on the first camera, and it headed over there where the second camera picked it up. I'll show you the next place.'

A few moments later they stood on the spot of the second and final sighting.

'It scampered off over there,' whispered Ted, waving his hand down a path that split into a junction at the end.

'You check out that path and I'll check out this one,' Mr Davis whispered placing his hand on Ted's shoulder.

'Would you like to come with me, Ted?'

Mr Davis slipped his hand into his coat pocket and pulled out something that resembled a mobile phone or bar code reader. Bending down he placed it near the ground. Studying the readout for a moment he then stood up.

'Nothing.'

'What's that little gizmo then?' asked Ted, craning his neck trying to get a better view of the mysterious scanner.

'Ah, clever stuff this. It should pick up the minute scent left by the little animal, no need for sniffer dogs now Ted.'

'Yea, but doesn't it get mixed up with any of the wildlife that lurks here over night like mice, squirrels, foxes, dare I say, rats?'

'No, it's scent discriminating, something to do with biochemical uniqueness of skin lipids or the like, that is unique human scent...'

Mr Davis hesitated, turned to look at Ted who stood there bewildered. Mr Davis hid his discomfort with a smirk and chuckled.

'What am I talking about? A unique animal scent.'

'OVER HERE!' shouted Mr Bill from the bird and pet area.

The two ran along the path and found Mr Bill bending over in a gap between two large rabbit hutches. He turned and beckoned Mr Davis over.

'Check this out. Look, there's a few prints there and several over there. I've got a reading on both and it looks like Z-006 and F-010. They must have spent some time here. The odd thing is that F-010 didn't appear to leave the area its footprints end right here.'

Ted stood up and scratched his head.

'Foot… footprints? Er, animals have paws, lads… ah, I suppose technically monkeys have feet and not paws though, eh?'

Mr Bill snapped, 'What was here?'

Pointing to an area of flattened yellow grass.

Ted nodded.

'That was one of our rabbit hutches, went out this morning.'

'Went out … What do you mean, went out?' asked Mr Davis straightening up.

'Delivered, bought last weekend and on the books for delivery first thing this morning. Why?'

Ted stuttered, looking confused.

Back in the office Ted ran his finger though the delivery book.

'There you go. Noddy and Andy are running it over to Cappelfield right now. 5, Victoria Road a Mrs Fen… OUCH… what the?'

Ted slapped his hand to the back of his neck and spun around in his chair.

'What was that?'

'Looked like a wasp or hornet to me. I tried to wave it away but the brute got you,' said Mr Bill, pretending to swat and follow the culprit out of the door with his eyes while slipping a small aluminium phial into his coat pocket.

'Flippin' things, I had a work colleague who was allergic to them and died hours after he was stung.'

Mr Davis cracked an unnatural smile.

'Well, Ted, you've been a great help and we'll give you a call to let you know the outcome and of course pay you for your time and help. I'll be handing you a nice fat brown envelope tomorrow morning. Oh, and I'd put an ice cube on that if I were you. Where's the kitchen?'

As Ted stood up and walked out of the office followed by Mr Davis, Mr Bill picked up and placed the delivery book back onto the shelf and ejected the tape from the CCTV player. He then took the business card that Ted had left by the telephone and dropped them into his coat pocket.

The two men left Ted in the kitchen attending his sting, and as they slowly walked past Pauline at the checkout, they bade farewell. Mr Bill turned to Mr Davis and ensuring Pauline could hear, said in a matter-of-fact air.

'Well, I think the storeroom extension plan looks reasonable, as long as its sympathetic to the existing buildings I can't see a problem.'

'Hope Mr Trevor's, OK, very nasty sting that.'

'Did you see the size of the thing? I hate wasps and hornets.'

His thin lips twisted into a sardonic smile.

The two men's apparent lack of haste walking out of the shop seemed odd as their big black 4x4 accelerated rapidly out of the car park kicking up dust and spraying gravel everywhere.

Some minutes later, Ted, clasping a bag of ice to his swollen neck staggered up to Pauline and mumbled,

'Pauline, I think I've had a bad reaction to a sting, hope I'm not allergic don't think I am but, ooh, don't feel well at all. I'm just going for a sit down in the office if you need me.'

Pauline stood up and asked if there was anything she could do but Ted just waved her back down into her seat and trudged away.

'I'll be all right in a mo.'

Half an hour later Pauline took Ted a nice mug of tea and a couple of rich tea biscuits. She found him slumped over his desk, head resting on arms.

A string of saliva hung from the corner of his open mouth forming a milky puddle on the desk. His eyes were wide open, almost bulging.

The mug and biscuits fell to the floor with a crash.

Ted was dead.

Chapter Six

It seemed an age before the garden centre van pulled up and parked. The two men jumped down from the cab.

Max craned his neck down and watched their boots stomp around to the rear of the van. They started unlatching the tailgate then a deafening crash as it dropped down, followed by a thunder-like rumble over Max's head as Flea's hutch was pulled to the open back of the van.

The two men walked up the drive of a large red brick house to the front door.

Max lowered himself down and darted under the tailgate of the van, cupped his hands together and in a loud whisper called,

'Flea… Flea, I'm here.'

There was a muffled excited response from Flea.

Max turned and quickly climbed back onto the spare wheel bracket as the two men returned.

One at each end, the two staggered up the drive with the hutch. Max dropped down again and hid behind the rear wheel. He peered around to see the two pause halfway up the drive. A rotund woman wearing a floral apron, clutching in her yellow rubber gloved hands a large blue bottle of bleach directed them around the side of the house towards the back garden.

Max vaulted up the kerb onto the pavement and scampered through the open gate and leapt amongst the shrubs to the side. He made his way along the fence keeping the trio in sight. Their boots on the gravel drive made such a din that Max didn't worry about avoiding treading on dry leaves or sticks.

Halfway up the garden under a large apple tree the woman boomed at them to place the hutch down.

'Just here thank you, so that the front faces the house.'

The younger man's grip slipped and his end of the hutch dropped onto his knees. Max flinched as he could imagine Flea falling out of the raised sleeping compartment and tumbling down onto the wire base of the hutch. What a shock they would all have if they saw her. She would be trapped within the cage while friends of the woman, her neighbours, children and everyone in the vicinity came to see the little freak human girl. How would the "OV" organisation explain that one away? Would they attempt to kill all these people? Yes, in a word. He wouldn't put it past them.

While the group had their backs turned Max scrambled as close as he dared to.

Three excited children ran and skipped from the house to their mother. The eldest of the two men bent down and to Max's horror unlatched the door to the cage. He swung the door open and partially closed it again as if showing the group how a hinged door worked!

Max spotted Flea's face tentatively peering around the entrance to the raised sleeping compartment. She looked like she was about to make a bolt for it.

The group moved to the back of the hutch and the elder man began to remove an access panel to the sleeping compartment. He paused and looked at the three children giving Flea enough time to scramble down the ramp and hide under it.

'And who's going to oversee cleaning out the rabbits then?'

They all answered in unison, 'I AM.'

All six bent down at the back of the hutch to look inside the compartment and at that point Flea jumped up, squeezed through the unlatched front door and ran as fast as she could away from the hutch.

Max was amazed at her speed. Her track took her straight to the side of the house. She threw herself behind a large black wheelie bin. Max turned expecting at least one of the groups to jump up having spotted her but no, phew, no.

'And we'll be buying a big bag of straw for their bed when we pick up the bunnies, won't we, Mummy?' came a little muffled voice.

'And food for them I hope,' answered the mother with a chuckle.

Max bending low behind the shrubbery and plants, moved cautiously towards the wheelie bin and managed to attract Flea's attention with a "Psst" and wave.

She crouched, holding her chest with both hands out of breath and panting, more likely from the adrenaline rush than the run.

Within minutes they were both together sitting behind a big conifer in a dark corner of the front garden. Max squeezed her hands and couldn't contain his joy.

'One day we'll be able to stand up dance and shout at the top of our voices for joy Flea, without a care in the world. No more stooping over every time we move, throwing ourselves to the ground to hide, no more running, just freedom to live in our own community hidden from the world.'

The two watched the men wave goodbye as they walked through the gate. Almost as soon as the van drove away, a large black Mercedes 4x4 pulled up outside the house. Max and Flea crouched down.

Two stern-looking men walked up the drive towards the front door. One rang the doorbell while the other made his way around the side of the house to the garden.

The mother answered the front door.

'Ah, madam, I'm Mr Reynolds from Lark-Hills Estate agents. We have an appointment with you to have a look at the property, take a few dimensions and photographs.'

The woman raised her hands, palms up and shaking her head answered.

'Sorry, I'm afraid you must have the wrong house we have absolutely no plans to move.'

Max had his eye on the man that walked through to the back garden. He was taking a good look at the new rabbit hutch. Seeing it was empty, he pulled a strange looking device from his coat pocket and seemed to be scanning the ground. Stooping over he followed the track Flea had taken to the wheelie bin.

'Oh no, it's them, it's them, they're on to us.'

Max grabbed Flea by the arm and on hands and knees they scrambled straight for a gap in the fence.

As both squeezed through the fence, they heard the man at the door apologise explaining it must be the other large house up the road, then called his colleague who he claimed with a strained laugh, was already looking over the premises at the back of the house.

From the neighbouring front garden and well hidden, Max and Flea strained their ears to listen to the two men standing out in the road by their Mercedes 4x4.

The man who had investigated the hutch shook his head.

'Wow, that was close. I thought it was going to be an X-3 for a moment there.'

'It's here or close, it must be, the scent was heavy around the hutch so it must have been in there because the hutch door showed a high reading.'

'It was F-010 and seemed to lead from the hutch towards a wheelie bin. Guess the reading was corrupted as I got to the bin because some silly germ fearing individual had sprinkled disinfectant or bleach around it.'

'Right, call in Echo-three now and get them to check out this area with a fine-tooth comb and set up a two-kilometre cordon to the south. We must catch it immediately and God knows where Z-006 is. We must try and catch at least one of the little pests alive and find out what their big plan is. Why are the ones that have been spotted moving south? I'd love to know.'

Max looked at Flea in disbelief.

'Catch at least one alive. Who had been killed? Were they the only survivors moving south? Good news though, to hear they didn't know the reason behind the march south.'

They had to move fast and get as far away from the area as possible and certainly not in a southerly direction now. The pair agreed to head west-north-west, keeping the midday sun just behind their left shoulders for the next few days, or at least until they were well beyond the cordon to the south.

Both scrambled silently away through the vegetation around the side of the neighbour's house and headed towards the back of the garden.

Flea turned to Max and whispered,

'That's so, so nice, shows that the establishment really did care about us, oh, and it does suit you, Max.'

Max looked confused.

'What suits me?'

'Z-006 and I love the way we're described as, it and pests!'

Max frowned and shook his head.

Flea flicked the hair from her face her eyes revealing a confused expression.

'One of those men said he thought it was nearly an X-3. What did he mean, X-3?'

Max's eyes averted down in thought.

'OK, we're keeping on the move now day and night.'

Chapter Seven

In the afternoon of the following day the two found themselves taking a short but well-earned rest.

It had been an exhausting trek. Behind to the east-south-east, the two had witnessed an unusual amount of helicopter activity during the previous afternoon and through the night. Now though it seemed as if the search had been scaled down.

Looking down from a low ridge on the edge of a golf course, limbs aching, Max and Flea lay on their fronts chin resting on hands, munching away on a small pile of blackberries they had collected. They felt content now that they were together.

Fortunately, their planned route would take them along the north side of the golf course.

The two took this opportunity to select new wooden sticks for protection against aggressive animals and discuss the reality of their future. Were they dreaming of the impossible? Could there be a better long-term plan for the survivors? The south of England had the disadvantage for them of being heavily populated. The flip side of the coin was the small but un-maintained very dense wooded areas in the south. Would they be better off in a more remote area of let's say, France? The establishment would think they had simply disappeared and would never know they had gone and even if they had, how could they operate and hunt them without attracting suspicion?

Flea reminded Max that the French country people loved hunting wild boar and deer with their hunting dogs and searching for truffles in remote wooded areas.

'Oh, I'm not saying this doesn't need a lot of thinking about, Flea.' Max sighed, tying a knot in a blade of grass.

'CANADA! The wilderness, we could really live out there and we wouldn't even need to hide. We could build a hamlet in a clearing next to a fresh spring or brook with an allotment for vegetables and we could even breed small animals of some sort and have fresh meat.'

'BEARS!' said Max, sitting up and holding both hands paw-like to Flea's face as if to pretend to maul her.

'WOLVES!' said Flea, leaping at and catching Max off balance making him roll flat on his back.

Their laughter evolved into giggles as they sat together watching two distant figures pulling golf caddies up one of the fairways.

That night after the last golfers returned to the clubhouse and the golf course closed, Max and Flea slipped down to one of its nearest hazard ponds and took a well-deserved drink and soak. Hidden by tall reeds they playfully splashed each other and frolicked. When the two had had enough they crawled out shivering under the cautious red eyes of a pair of coots and dried themselves as best they could with dock leaves.

Moving back under cover, they made a bivouac of sticks dressed with moss in a dense thicket on the north west corner of the golf course.

It was a slightly alien looking site, as here and there peering out behind the thicket stems, the odd lost golf ball lay half buried in natural leaf mulch like toadstools from a distant planet.

The two ate some of the nut and berry rations collected on their trek that afternoon while sipping delicious raspberry juice squeezed into an acorn cup.

Dry, cosy, clean and safe, they both lay staring out of the bivouac entrance up through the rustling foliage to the night sky beyond talking about the events during the last twenty-four hours. The what ifs were interrupted by a bright shooting star zipping through the night sky. There was a tired half-hearted "Wow!" from both and then they fell into a deep sleep.

A day and a half trekking west and northwest, saw the two turn onto a southerly heading. They had made fairly good progress, but both felt that heading more than ninety degrees to their planned track and destination was hardly any progress at all. At the end of the day though all that extra effort and lost time was for deception and for their very survival.

'We need to get up high and see what lies to the south, it could save us days even weeks,' said Flea as she stood on tip toe to check whether the coast was clear to cross a country lane.

Max double checked and they scurried across, bent low like soldiers under fire.

As the two crawled through the hedgerow on the other side Max asked, 'How though? Do you know, I've often thought of climbing a church spire or tower for that reason even without the right equipment, but the chance of being caught would be far too high. Can you imagine going up the stair route and hearing someone climbing and stomping up the winding staircase towards you? Getting closer and closer as you try to heave yourself up one step at a time until exhausted, you wait until the vicar in a dog collar rounds the corner and there you are eye to eye.'

'Yes, I could,' said Flea smiling.

'I'd say in a sweet and innocent voice with my arms outstretched and slowly flapping like wings, 'Hello, vicar, I'm an angel and I've been sent to look at your church roof. You see from up there in heaven it really looks like you need to get some repairs done!'

'Nope, we need to climb an electricity pylon, and look over there.'

She straightened her back with a self-congratulatory air, pointing to a line of electricity pylons marching across the countryside.

'They must be at least sixty metres or more high and no fear of being trapped by someone.'

Max studied the closest pylon.

'Ah, I see, we could climb on all fours up the steel lattice work that crosses at an angle.'

Within a couple of hours, the two stood at the base of the massive structure planning their ascent.

Max raised his arm, thumb and forefinger open and closed one eye looking between both counting slowly.

He was measuring the estimated time it would take them to climb each lattice section and allowing for a rest after every two sections.

'No way!' he muttered, dropping his arms to his side, 'It's going to take roughly a day to climb and a day to get dorrrrrrrrrrrrrwn.'

'Not if we only climb as far as we need. There should be no need to go right to the very top. Anyway, I don't fancy getting zapped by the power up there,' said Flea placing her hand on his shoulder and pointing up to a red enamel sign with white lettering stating, "Danger 32,000 volts".

'We would have to begin the climb as soon as the light fades, stay up there during daylight and climb down tomorrow when night falls. Twenty-four hours is a long time to be hanging about up there, eh?'

Max looked around.

'It's pretty remote here Flea there's no footpath or building, nothing apart from a few cows over on that meadow we passed earlier. The fields around here have been left as set aside. Why not go for it tonight and as daylight breaks in the morning have a good scan around, then carefully start the descent early in daylight? We would be down by mid-morning. Nobody would spot us and if we tie grass onto our tops to break our silhouette and keep a really good look out, no one ever will. We'll just look like a crow's nest or something.'

Flea smiled and said this in an aristocratic voice as she lifted her right hand in a royal wave and made herself a comfortable throne on the grass to wait until sunset.

'Or, you lay down, my dearest, and pretend to be the nest and I could be the hen crow and stand on you and we'd look like a crow on her nest to any twitcher with their binoculars don't you think?'

'Brilliant idea my dear, absolutely top notch.'

Replied Max in an equally aristocratic voice, rocking back and forth stroking his chin.

As the sun dipped below the horizon in the west the two summoned their strength and prepared for the ascent.

They hid Max's rucksack and both their sticks at the base of one pylon leg.

'Are you ready to flout the safety guidelines?' grunted Max as he pulled himself up onto the rough concrete base of the pylon leg.

The most strenuous part of the climb was up the near vertical first broad leg to the horizontal barbed wire security fencing.

As soon as they had squeezed themselves through the barbed wire it was fairly straight forward but extremely tiring.

On hands and knees, they climbed at about forty-five degrees zig-zagging their way up in the milky moonlight.

The first rest stop saw them sitting astride a horizontal "I" beam at about nineteen metres above the ground.

They could see the moonlit fields stretching away into the distance, but they would have to climb much higher to be able to see over the tree tops in the daylight.

'Hey, no rush,' Max yelped when Flea's head bumped into his rear and nearly made him miss his hand hold as they climbed.

'We have all night and we want to be fit for the descent tomorrow'

By 2 a.m. they decided that they had climbed far enough and settled down as best they could.

With their backs pushed into a large junction bracket and sitting on the corner joint of two horizontal beams at the junction with the vertical column they managed to get fairly comfortable and secure.

The two found it virtually impossible to nod off for they knew that if they awoke forgetting for a moment where they were and shifting a couple of centimetres the wrong way would mean a plunge to their death.

Max was angry with himself for not collecting useful bits and pieces on their trek, a length of garden string, stuff like that always came in useful. At least they could have bound themselves to the upright and slept, maybe.

The pair sat and looked south. In that dim moonlight cornfields within less than five kilometres had a ghostly silver blue hew, while the green pasture meadows were a dark grey framed with black woodland and copses, beyond that total darkness apart from the light pollution created by a very large town to the southeast. The orange light gave a weak glow to the base of the clouds. It was difficult to say how far but they both agreed the town must be Basingstoke. If it wasn't, then they were not where they thought they were.

After an hour or so, the moon was blanked out by low clouds and the orange glow in the southeast became a fuzzy faint smudge. Sure, enough and as they thought within half an hour it began to drizzle.

The two pulled their legs up under their chins and cuddled up. Fortunately, the angle of the steel upright sheltered them to some extent.

As dawn came a grey featureless daylight spread across the countryside, Max and Flea were hugely disappointed to find the visibility was terrible. They had both assumed that because there was good visibility the previous day, this day would be the same. How stupid. All that effort for nothing.

Fortunately, it was mild so they decided to literally hang on and see if there would be an improvement through the morning. They would give it until midday and if the visibility had not improved, then they would climb down and head in the direction that would initially keep Basingstoke as best they could to their ten 'o clock position.

As they both sat whiling away the time, Max asked Flea, his breath visible in the damp air, what had been her earliest memory in the establishment?

'I guess it must have been at the very beginning of nursery school when we were taken up to surface level to play in the safe area. It was my first encounter with sunlight and it was blinding. They dressed us all in light green smocks with a florescent orange square patch on the back and we had huge floppy hats and tinted green lens goggles.

'I had never seen sand or grass before and was terrified of going near the grass.

'I remember looking at my carer for comfort and he stood above me writing notes on a clipboard. He then lifted me in the palm of his hand and dropped me into the grass which completely covered me so that I couldn't see the other children and I screamed and cried with fear until he lifted me out, held me up to his face and gave me a look over then put me on the sand and finished writing notes.

'I guess there are earlier memories but they don't stand out like that one because it was all… well, all very grey.'

Max looked into Flea's eyes and in a quiet voice said,

'I would say that was my very first memory too. The first visit to the top. I remember feeling a breeze on my face and I remember pointing to the sky in excitement. I wanted my carer to see the birds like the ones from my picture book flying along the big blue ceiling.'

'Did you have a favourite carer, Flea?'

Flea thought for a moment and then said she did, a carer called Lyn who was so much kinder than the others were.

Max agreed Lyn was a nice person at heart, but he believed that when she was exhibiting her friendship or sense of caring it was an act to fit in with the other personnel.

Lyn had told the group once when they were all sitting under a large willow tree in the safe zone and far too young to understand the real reason, the undercover military element. The project would eventually be used to reduce the size of all creatures on Earth in the fight against eventual worldwide overpopulation. Yes, the world would become a much, much larger place!

'Do you remember once we all had to do an IQ test under extreme conditions? As you know, it was calculated on the ratio of your mental age to your actual age, multiplied by one hundred, and my result was well under one hundred, it was just not my day, and I really didn't care either.

'Lyn took my papers looked through them with that magnifying glass thing she always checked our work with and seemed shocked. I remember her taking my papers to her desk then looking around and over her glasses at me, started to rub out and make alterations to my paperwork.

'Do you remember Flea after that IQ test Rip and Vizz disappeared? We were told they had gone to another region, but now I reckon that they were destroyed, given a lethal injection or something like that because maybe they didn't match up to the standard needed.'

'Rip and Vizz.'

Flea turned to Max with a look of disbelief.

He saw a look in her eyes he had never seen before.

'Vizz was the nice-looking boy with bright blue eyes, wasn't he?'

'Yes, personally I thought he was sort of odd and intense. Think about it, Flea. The two of them always seemed to finish first in mental tests and maybe they got it all wrong you know, too hurried. Great in physical tests though but it wasn't enough, was it?'

Flea looked down and shook her head slowly.

'God,' she whispered.

'Think about it Flea. If my memory serves me right, there were almost twice as many more of us attending nursery school in the four-year-old age group compared to the number of fifteen-year-olds in the establishment before we escaped.'

Flea nodded solemnly and whispered,

'I remember the look on Lyn's face the day after the two of them were sent away. She was definitely not herself for weeks. Remember her having a huge argument with one of the scientists and a couple of supervisors in the gym?'

'I do,' whispered Max, turning to look at her.

He reached out and squeezed her hand gently.

'And she disappeared for a month or so. She came back looking thin and drawn as if she hadn't slept for weeks but just carried on as normal.'

'Oh yes!' snarled Flea pulling her hand from his to hold her head in her hands.

'One of us asked how the two were getting on in their new region and asked where the new region was, do you remember?'

'You didn't see her reaction did you when the supervisor told us that they were only a block or so away with the young ones and doing really well?

'I don't think anyone else in the class saw it, but I noticed that she looked absolutely disgusted and walked out. At the time it made no sense to me but now it does.

'Those scheming, cold, callous, murdering monsters.'

With sullen faces they both sat deep in thought.

Since the rabbit hutch escape Max's mind kept returning to the comment one of the men made.

'Whoa, that was close. I thought it was going to be an X-3 for a moment there.'

With a flash something clicked in Max's memory.

A file he and Puk found during one of their covert play games. The two had climbed through an air vent into the psychology unit one night for a look-around and took great pleasure finding an unlocked safe with a file inside.

The file was titled "X-1 to three" and the contents of it covered experimentation using hypnosis and its use in covert operations. There were three categories in the file but until now Max and Puk could not make sense of what they read. There was a reference to named and imprisoned violent psychiatric patients and articles on gunmen who had gone berserk in towns and villages in the UK, Europe and the rest of the world. This was not unusual for the establishment because they had to understand and get into the minds of terrorists or enemies of the state. However, why A4 plans of these high security hospitals with highlighter rings around doors and perimeter fences?

It all seemed a bit of a bore at the time because there was plenty of fun to be had elsewhere, like the complex executive office toy on the desk for instance.

Max shuddered with realisation.

'Cold?' asked Flea, half turning pulling her cuffs over her hands.

Max knew instinctively he should not share this realisation or theory with Flea, well not yet.

He now thought he knew why that file existed.

Back at that house, if Flea had been discovered and trapped within the rabbit hutch before it was too late and too many neighbours had called to witness the living fairy, followed by a call to the local newspaper, the village would have had a visit. First, rapidly on the scene the two men in the black Mercedes 4x4 would have grabbed Flea and fled.

Followed by a rapid drop off, a phone call or click of the thumb and finger and one of their pre-hypnotised and ever ready crazed gunman, or, as they called them the last resort, an X-3 would tidy up.

The two sat in silence, staring into nothing for what seemed an age until Max nudged Flea and pointed to two small Muntjac deer far below trotting along together, stopping every now and again to lift their heads, looking around and sniffing the air to make sure there were no predators about.

'We must develop a greater sense of smell like those deer, Flea for our survival, eh,' Max said uncomfortably reaching slowly across to hold her shivering cuff covered hand.

By midday the visibility had improved slowly enough to see at least fifteen to twenty kilometres. Enough distance to study the landscape to the south.

Unfortunately, the weak midday sun was high to the south which didn't help the distant detail. The two of them squinting and shading their eyes focused on the area to the right of Basingstoke where Cork's airfield was supposed to be located.

'Look!' whispered Max excitedly, 'Look, I think I saw a glint over there in the sky, look there it is again. I'm sure it's an aeroplane turning.'

Flea carefully stood up as if those few centimetres would give her a better view.

'I've got it yes. Do you think it's near Cork's airfield Copham Max?'

'Well, it must be close to Cork's airfield I reckon. Let's get a good bearing from here check out distant landmarks to look for on the ground like that church spire way over there and climb down.'

Max sounded the most enthusiastic Flea had ever heard.

They stood side by side looking and pointing to the south, mentally recording barns, masts, woods and hills.

Happy they had all landmarks recorded they prepared to descend the pylon.

Max went first and as he climbed down onto the first angled cross member on hands and knees, he looked up at Flea to warn her that the metalwork was wet with last night's drizzle and incredibly slippery now.

Flea watched in horror as his face seemed to diminish in scale. He was sliding away and down the cross member at forty-five degrees gaining speed still on all fours. Throwing his face and chest flat with arms and legs wrapped as far as he could manage around the steelwork, he did not slow down. Max careered away from Flea until he hit the upright steelwork below with such a force that his back and head were thrown back against it. Flea watched on in horror as Max sat upright for a moment then slumped slowly to his right disappearing from her view.

Flea screamed louder than she had ever screamed in her whole life.

She clambered onto the angled cross member pulling her grass camouflage under her and slid down gaining speed with her feet ready to take the impact against the upright steelwork.

She crashed with a loud crack against it, her legs taking the force.

Seeing the fingers of Max's left hand grasping the edge of the horizontal beam she thrust herself sideways and grabbed his wrist just in time. Max hung there limp, head flopped down over his chest with Flea holding on for dear life. Her hands were wet and she could feel her grasp slipping so she dug her nails into Max's flesh as hard as she could.

After what seemed an age, Max twitched and came around fully with his head jerking up in instant realisation at the predicament they were in. He swung his right arm up with his fingers grabbing the lower edge of the "I" beam.

Flea was not going to let go but she could feel herself slipping around the beam slowly and in doing so, looked down into the tangled steel latticework framed abyss. A rush of acrophobia surged through her making her squeeze her eyes tight shut, it was as if she would prefer to fall into the vertiginous depths than hang on in that impossible situation.

Max's voice shook her out of it.

'HOLD ON, FLEA I'm OK, I think. Just got to get...'

His face came up to hers then his leg lifted over the beam, he rolled himself over on top of her legs puffing and gasping for air.

Flea threw her head back and let out a scream of pain.

'My leg, my leg, I think it's broken.'

Max lifted himself onto his hands as best he could taking his weight off her legs.

'Which leg?' he panted.

Flea grimaced and moved her left hand shakily down over her thigh to her left lower leg.

The two were exhausted and stayed for a couple of minutes almost frozen in that position gasping for breath.

When Max had regained his breath, he gingerly positioned himself to take a looked at her left leg. The leg seemed to be straight which was a good sign. He ran his hand down her leg from below the knee and as he got to her ankle, she let out a yelp. He carefully pulled up her trouser leg and felt her ankle.

'I think it's a sprain or you've twisted it Flea.'

They both manoeuvred themselves carefully into a safer more comfortable position wedged between the cross member and upright.

Flea turned to Max looking very pale and whispered shakily,

'That was close.'

'Thanks Flea it was your voice that brought me around. If you hadn't shouted and grabbed me, I'd be down there now.'

He tilted his head to the drop.

'How am I going to get down? I'm afraid to move and I won't be able to stand or crawl on this leg,' she whimpered almost in tears.

'We'll think of something.'

He placed his arm around her and gave her a hug.

'We made enough noise to raise an army,' he chuckled.

Nervously scanning the fields below, they decided to stay sitting like that until the wet steelwork dried off in the sun.

By late afternoon early evening the two prepared themselves once again for an attempt to descend. This was going to take forever, and it did. Flea's ankle and new height phobia being a big problem.

The two developed a system that would have looked like two caterpillars wriggling along but it worked and was safe. The worst part for Flea was the climb down to the next cross brace and there were about nine in all.

Easily the most difficult moment was the last vertical descent through the barbed wire and down the leg of the pylon. Flea had to climb onto Max's back holding on with her right arm over his shoulder, grasping her left hand that passed under his arm to prevent choking him.

At last puffing and panting, both made that final step onto terra firma.

Max dropped onto all fours and kissed the ground, then examined his sore, raw hands. Flea hopped a couple of times then slumped onto her back in the wet grass groaning in relief. Max rolled over to Flea. She turned pointing her finger to his nose saying, in a firm and rather unfriendly voice.

'Can I be frank with you?'

Max now greatly relieved, gasping for air replied,

'If you like, but Frank's a bit masculine and doesn't suit you. Flea's a much nicer name for a gir…'

Flea cut him short and snapped.

'Don't you ever, ever suggest we climb one of those horrible things again.'

Max taken aback by the abruptness of the demand raised both hands to the sky and in a despairing voice uttered,

'It was you who… oh, never mind.'

Chapter Eight

To hop slowly with one arm over Max's shoulder for support
was about the only way Flea could move. Realising the trek
south would be impossibly slow now the two decided to rest
up for however long it took for her ankle to get better.
Between the two of them though, there was an unspoken fear
of autumn arriving before they reached Cork's airfield, their
destination.

From up the pylon the two had spotted the ivy-covered
derelict remains of an old plough shed on the west side of the
neighbouring meadow and it looked remote. The shed was
hardly a structure at all just two crumbling upright brick walls
and the rest, a tangled mess of rotting roof beams and slate.

After staggering, stumbling, and tripping their way
through high grass and the odd thistle the pair arrived at the
remains. Flea sat outside while Max surveyed the sheds
interior.

The pair decided that they would make camp inside the
walls and under the fallen roof. The floor was hard dusty earth
and the shafts of golden light from the evening sun made the
floor look like gold leaf. Age-old matted cobwebs hung above
their heads like tatty theatre drapes.

Max dragged small lengths of timber and slate over to the
corner and made an inner structure with half brick seats
covered with moss and a dry grass bed, framed with broken
roof slats. Flea helped when she could but this just annoyed
Max.

'Rest your leg. Sit there and put your leg up on that brick please,' he barked every now and again as he caught her hopping about.

'This will do just for tonight. I'll make it a lot more presentable in the morning for our stay until you can walk properly,' he muttered under his breath as he rolled an old rusty tin on its side and bent down to light a fire inside it using his small lighter, dry leaves and flakes of dry rotten wood.

The tin soon heated up nicely. Max placed their damp clothing close to the heat to dry and settled down for the night with some ground up nuts to eat and berries to suck the juice from. The pair now totally exhausted, flexed their stiff limbs and were just getting comfortable, sitting there staring at the wisps of smoke wafting up from the small fire into the darkness when a small, yellow-necked mouse poked his head through a small break in the brickwork and crept in showing interest in their camp. The mouse hadn't seen the pair sitting motionless and sniffed around he caught Flea's gaze, froze and studied her for half a second, turned, and as quick as a flash scampered away into the darkness sending up a cloud of fine dust.

Flea turned to Max her face lit up with a broad smile and whispered,

'Aww sweet! It must have been the warmth from the fire, Max. Wouldn't it be just lovely to have her as a pet?'

Max smiled back and nodded in agreement.

'She was very cute. I don't for one minute believe she'd curl up in a ball at our feet though. How's the leg?'

'It's throbbing at the moment but so nice to put it up and rest.'

Flea sighed looking down at the fire light dancing shadows on her leg and trying to fight off sleep.

With the embers of the fire still glowing and the hoot of a pair of owls in the distance, the two retired to bed and snuggled up for the night knowing they were in an isolated safe and secure place for once.

By the end of the next day Max had managed to make this place something special. That morning he had squeezed out through a large crack at the back corner of the shed and almost fallen headfirst into a small brook that flowed crystal clear beside the wall. This discovery was better than he could have hoped for with fresh drinking water so close.

Max washed their clothing, watched like a hawk by Flea sitting within the cracked wall giving instructions every now and then.

'Do under the arms well. Don't stir up the mud.'

He was glad to complete the task and hung the clothing out carefully to dry over twigs.

That evening the two ate baked stickleback. Max had managed, with much hilarity, to catch five of the little fish using a length of old sacking found in the ruins to make a funnel trap and had encased them in clay to cook. The taste was a little bitter and for a small fish very bony, but they enjoyed every morsel.

Flea wiped the grease off her lips with the back of her hand.

'Do you know what I've missed?'

'No, what?'

'That fine bread we used to have at the establishment, I've really missed bread. Have you, Max?'

'Yep, bread would have gone down really well with that supper. That's one thing we can't make living out here in the wild.'

Flea screwed her nose up at him.

'I wouldn't call this living wild Max. This is cosy and isolated, and we even have running water at the back.'

Max nodded in agreement. He knew they were lucky to find such a place when they did.

Before coming in with the fish he had glanced up at the milky sky, a sure sign of plenty of rain to come.

Flea had a restless night. Her sprained ankle had throbbed constantly; however, she finally fell asleep around dawn so Max left her in peace and decided to go out berry and nut hunting. He crawled through to the front of the shed but changed his mind about going out when he saw rain falling from the leaden sky. He made himself comfortable on a tuft of dry grass, just under the shelter of the fallen roof and listened to the pitter-patter of rain on the slates above his head. Rivulets of water ran along and disappeared through the gaps in the old moss-covered flagstones. Max pulled his knees up under his chin and enjoyed this moment. Time to relax.

He had been with Flea constantly and without a break for days, although it seemed like weeks. It was nice to sit and be alone for a while, just left to his own thoughts. Max knew all too well the horrible loneliness he had felt before finding Flea. He would never forget that isolation, but this was nice. Just a couple of hours to sit and think on his own. After the first hour of sitting there, Max realised he had not really thought about anything at all, he had been in a daydream, tossing blades of dry grass into the rivulets of rainwater and watching them float away.

Max must have nodded off for a moment. When he woke, he felt cold and slightly groggy. Rain was now pounding loudly on the slates above and water was up to the base of his grass tuft seat. The strong smell of damp vegetation pleasantly assaulted his nostrils.

'Well, I'd better see how Flea is,' Max muttered as he stretched his arms, yawned and straightened up.

He hesitated for a moment as his bleary eyes focused on something odd about the dry dusty floor back into their hide. A damp smeared track two centimetres wide curved left and right from the outside into the darkness, it was almost as if Flea had got up, gone out into the rain and dragged something inside. But why?

She would have woken me for sure and she couldn't have missed me. She'll be soaked through.

Max stooped under the fallen timbers and followed the damp track into the shadows.

His eyes acclimatised to the dark and what he saw shook him to the bone and he froze. Flea was fast asleep, she hadn't moved at all but lying beside the bed with its chin resting on one corner next to her head was a large snake, an Adder with its grey/brown coloured body and a very distinctive black zigzag pattern on its back. Max knew that if she woke and lashed out, the snake would either recoil and slither away or bite. The venom would be fatal for them at their size.

He remembered that Adders would disappear into the bushes and undergrowth quickly if they felt vibrations of a threat approaching but this was in a very confined space. It had obviously come into the dry as its habitat was possibly flooding in the rain.

The snake did not seem to realise Max was standing there and to his horror it flicked a black glistening forked tongue along Flea's arm as if sensing another living creature.

Flea shrugged, rolled over onto her side with her back to the snake.

'Stop it Max... don't... it's not funny,' she grumbled through an indolent yawn.

Max decided that the best course of action would be to distract the snake and try to get it to focus on him without waking Flea. Max tip toed carefully, pausing at each step over to their belongings and reached out for his stick. As his fingers touched the stick the snake reacted to his movement and slowly turned its head side-on to him, the black orbs of its eyes showed no sign of fear or anger.

Max froze again, he was in a real state of fear and strangely finding himself admiring this proud-looking beast.

Flea stirred and muttered into her pillow of dry grass.

'Max... I'm starving... I could eat a...'

She turned her head expecting Max to be sitting on the edge of the bed.

'... a SNAKE.'

She spun away and fell onto the floor on the other side of the makeshift bed.

'STAY THERE, DON'T MOVE!' shouted Max as he grabbed the stick and held it Kendo style towards the Adder.

'Stay still, Flea, it's an Adder not a grass snake. Whatever you do don't move.'

Max stepped clear of any escape route the Adder could take, their eyes were fixed on each other.

The black forked tongue appeared again and sampled the air then its head slowly recoiled taking its upper body with it as if retreating. The snake's back end slid into a tighter coil. For several seconds the two stayed perfectly still as if trapped in a time warp.

Compared to Max the thing was like a giant Boa Constrictor. The difference being that this beast would move a lot quicker.

'What's going on, Max?'

'I don't know it's just… it's just looking at me… oh, it's on the move.'

Its head moved from side to side as if judging distance then like a flash of lightning the Adder struck. Max threw himself to the right.

The Adders mouth thumped into its prey; its teeth sunk into the flesh with such force that it made a sickening ripping sound that penetrated the loud squeal of shock from its victim. Blood spat in two lines onto the dusty floor.

Flea curled into a ball, covered her face and screamed through her hands. To add to the terror, she heard something approaching at speed. It grabbed her arm like a clamp. With her eyes tightly shut, she lashed out with her clenched fist. There was good hard impact. Max slumped down on top of her unconscious.

Flea struggled out from beneath Max, kicked the slate bedroom shelter wall away, grabbed his arms and pulled with all her might into the tangled mess of rotting timber and sacking. The adrenaline rush completely masked the pain from her ankle.

As she struggled with Max she nervously checked for the Adder's whereabouts. There it was, near the place Max had stood with his stick. In its mouth was the twitching body of the small, yellow-necked mouse that had entertained Flea and Max that first night.

Flea backed herself and Max between two fallen timbers. At least she could defend herself and Max here by kicking out at the beast if it approached.

Max started to come around. His head rolled drunkenly from side to side, then as if hit by an electric shock, jerked his arms and legs out straight.

'What the… where is it? Where are we?'

He turned his head and looked at her.

'It's OK. Sorry Max, I really thought you were the snake.'

Max lifted his hand and rubbed the side of his head.

'That's twice I've been knocked out now in the space of a week.'

'Did you see he got our mouse?' whispered Flea as she strained her neck to see if there was any movement in their sleeping quarters.

'I did, poor thing. They must have both come in from the rain. Goodness knows what else will be visiting, could turn into a zoo in here. I can tell you Flea, if that thing had come at me, I wouldn't have stood a chance, it sprang so fast.'

The two stayed wedged between the fallen timbers for several hours. Every now and again they heard slight movement from their quarters.

'I think we have to find another way out of here Flea. That snake could stay for days now that it's eaten something.'

The two decided that they could not leave their possessions behind as they were all in the other area, coats, rucksacks, sticks and most importantly, food and their dwindling supply of nourishment pills.

The next morning long after the rain had stopped, they glimpsed the Adder move out, the smooth enamel-like skin glistening as it slowly slid away in the direction it had entered.

Flea stood wobbling on one leg as she massaged her ankle and peered up into the derelict remains of the shed roof.

Stomp... stomp... shuffle... stomp.

Max's muffled voice came down from above.

'It's good up here. There's a sizeable flat area and it's pretty stable.'

Max had climbed up a fallen roof joist and found a safe place for however long Flea's ankle took to heal.

'OK but ... don't snakes climb?'

'Well… yes, but at least we'll have the upper hand up here wont we?'

Max let out a loud frustrated sigh and a not so loud 'For snake's sake!'

On the morning of the third day Flea decided she was fit to carry on with their trek southward. She emphasised the point armed with a crutch Max had made for her by marching up and down as best she could in front of him.

'Well, I'm not getting those stabbing pains like I had.'

'I know Flea, but what if we get caught in a compromising situation out in the open for instance?' asked Max, stroking his chin and frowning in quiet desperation as he visualised a possible scenario in his mind's eye.

Flea straightened up and barked,

'What? Like I did when I knocked you out and dragged you to safety when our visitor came the other day?'

'Fair comment. I'll get the stuff together then,' muttered Max through a half smile.

Chapter Nine

Flea now set the pace as best she could with her limp and crutch, Max followed several paces behind. Both were slipping and sliding since sunrise along the rain-drenched field boundaries.

They enjoyed and soaked up the first rays of warm sunshine having been cooped up in the ruined plough shed for what seemed like weeks.

The sounds of a beautiful sunny morning were evident all around, with fieldfares and larks twittering above, bees buzzing by and the not so natural sound of the drone of a light aircraft or two overhead.

The pair trudged on their feet clad in heavy sticky mud. Every now and again a little waft of steam rose from their damp clothing.

Max would stop every half hour.

'Right Flea, rest please. I can see you're having trouble.'

Flea picked a buttercup with both hands and held it up to her face and smiled as she admired the bright yellow flower then set it down gently.

'I'm fine honestly. Don't worry, I'll stop when I need to.'

Max watched her wobble on and frowned.

'Better stubborn and hardy than feeble I guess.'

A day and a half later saw the two approach a small hamlet with caution to try and acquire more salt, cereals, sugar and fingers crossed, chocolate. It would have to be another risky kitchen raid.

They positioned themselves beneath a well-trimmed sweet-smelling cypress hedge, pulled off their rucksacks and settled down to watch through a huge well-maintained cobweb across a well-kept garden to the rear of a small picturesque, thatched cottage.

Flea gave a thumbs up to Max and whispered, 'Ah, great no children's toys and there's a cat flap in the back door.'

'Have you done this before Flea?'

'This will be my third kitchen operation, well that's not strictly true. One was an allotment shed, but it was well stocked with packets of crisps and stuff, oh, and enough horrible beer and spirits to open an off licence!'

They lay there for half an hour watching. With no sign of life in or outside the cottage Max nudged Flea's arm.

'Do you know what a gnome is?'

Flea turned and looked quizzically at Max.

'Yes of course, why?'

'Oh, nothing just wondered. Right, it's not worth the two of us taking the risk. You wait here and rest your leg. I'll be back in a while.'

Not waiting for a reply Max pulled his moss cloak over his shoulders picked up his rucksack and stick, then crawled slowly out on all fours and kept within cover of the hedge and abundant flower bed.

Flea watched like a hawk, she caught glimpses of him as he made his way slowly around the edge of the garden and approached the back door of the cottage. He carefully pushed the cat flap and it opened a little. Max turned towards Flea and raised his thumb. She watched as he stealthily opened the flap, peered inside for a moment to check all was clear then slipped through the opening.

Now it was a matter of waiting until he appeared hopefully with a nice fat bag of goods.

Max found himself in a tiny dark-beamed kitchen with a grey flagstone floor. There was a slight aroma of boiled cabbage and scented candles.

To his relief, a small cat food bowl and well abused catnip mouse lay by a large pair of green Wellington boots standing neatly inside the back door. Something told him that this cottage was inhabited by an elderly couple. He felt guilty. Surely, they wouldn't mind him taking tiny morsels to survive on. He only wished he could walk up to them, introduce himself and ask but they would most probably faint or stamp on him.

Max crouched by the boots and listened. There was a radio playing sombre classical music in what must be the lounge and a steady low tick-tock from a red-framed clock on the kitchen wall. Other than that, no sign of life.

After waiting cautiously for several minutes Max crept over to explore the base cabinets. He wouldn't risk climbing up onto the worktops but would open the lower units one by one.

With a heave Max opened the first unit door enough to peer in. A bucket, scrubbing brush and various containers of cleaning fluid. The next revealed several tins of cat meat and a small, opened carton of cat biscuits which he would return to if no other food was found.

Max crept across to what looked like a larder door just beyond the picture-magnet encrusted fridge.

A tiny gap allowed him to place his fingers in and pull.

The door creaked a little as it opened making Max wince, but inside shelves of goodies. He slipped through the gap and pulled the door back as it had been behind him and winced again as this time the un-oiled hinges gave a higher pitched creak.

Not wanting to climb up, he peered at the goods on the lower shelves. Under the first shelf were three small newspaper-lined wooden boxes containing potatoes, onions and runner beans.

On the first shelf stood a bag of sugar, a bumper bag of crisps and, excellent, two packets of breakfast cereals. Max would have to pull himself up onto one of the wooden boxes and then up onto the first shelf. He hid his stick and moss coat by the side of a box, threw his bag up onto the shelf and climbed up.

As he pulled himself onto the top edge of the box Max slipped on the newspaper lining. He bent down to pull the paper away. As he did so he focused on the title of an article.

Max stepped onto the potatoes within the box and being careful not to tear the newspaper, hurriedly pulled three small potatoes away then straightened out the creases in the paper.

Tilting his head, he read in a whisper to himself.

"Fairy couple tragically die."

Max swept crumbs of dry earth from the paper with the back of his hand.

"Mr and Mrs Forman, the couple who claimed to have encountered fairies at the bottom of their garden were tragically killed in a hit and run accident while walking their pet Labrador Toby who also died."

Max let out a muted gasp and read on.

"The driver of the unidentified vehicle possibly a dark-coloured 4x4 is being sought by the police. If anyone witnessed a vehicle being driven at speed along Harp Lane or around the village of Parford last Thursday, please contact Hampshire Police on 0800 555 1155.

'The Formans' contacted the *Hampshire Daily Echo* last week after claiming to have had a very strange encounter with two living doll-sized girls. They agreed at the time it would appear to be a very far-fetched story but were adamant the encounter was true. Toby the Labrador even had scars on his nose to prove the encounter they claimed.

Were these tiny beings, fairies? More like aggressive little female goblins the couple agreed!"

Max straightened the top of the newspaper out and looked at the date then laid the paper down gently in a gesture of remorse.

Poor things. I wonder who they were? They said two girls. It could have been Kat and Ali. Those monsters made sure the

97

Formans' tale went no further than a small article in the local paper.

Max jumped down from the box and peered through the gap in the larder door to the red-framed clock in the kitchen. The date window on the face of the clock showed that the newspaper was about three weeks old. Max turned back to the shelves.

I wish I knew where Parford was.

Within minutes, Max had filled his rucksack with breakfast cereals and a quantity of sugar.

He lowered the weighty rucksack down onto the potato-filled box and climbed down.

Max froze as he peered out through the gap in the larder door. A telephone rang abruptly in the hallway.

'Get that, love, Bertie's fast asleep on my lap.'

Max watched as a kind-looking, smartly dressed grey-haired elderly lady shuffled out of the lounge in her oversized slippers to the telephone.

'Hello, the Russells.'

She stood listening for a moment carefully adjusting flowers in an arrangement on the telephone table.

'Yes, and I told a gentleman from your company just the other day that we don't need a free site survey.

'I know he said there was an epidemic in this area, but I can promise you, my husband and I have not seen one rodent, rat, mouse or, what did your man say, ah, non-native Agouti at all. Even the crumbs under the bird table are still there in the morning!'

She stood listening examining her nails.

'No, perfectly all right, goodbye.'

She shuffled back into the lounge and out of site.

'Those silly people have given us more trouble than the dammed rodents they are after!'

The husband piped up.

'Mrs Westcott was going on about the darn rodent business this morning at the post office and those escaped wotsit's from that private collection or flippin zoo! If it's not climate change, it's rodents. Don't know what the world's coming too it's all hype and panic nowadays... oh Bertie, bad boy... he's just blown off again dear.'

There was a rustle of newspaper pages and all went quiet.

Flea sighed with relief as she watched a bulging rucksack plop onto the path beneath the cat-flap followed immediately by Max. Once out he grabbed the rucksack turned right, hugging the cottage wall and scampered into the nearest flower bed.

Eventually he joined her placing the rucksack down between them. She knew Max well and was expecting to be filled in on the details of the mission immediately but instead Flea noticed no smile and a look of sadness in his eyes.

'What's up? You OK?'

Max swept his hair away from his eyes and looked back at the house.

'Interesting, they are stepping up the search Flea. I found a three-week-old local newspaper too. You wouldn't believe the article. Two of "us" spotted in a garden, two girls. Must have been Kat and Ali. The couple who spotted them were killed in a hit and run accident a few days later. It stated, possibly a dark-coloured 4x4. We know who that could have been.'

Flea thumped the ground with her fist.

Max went on to describe the article and phone call in detail.

Flea looked into Max's eyes with an icy glare.

'They're getting away with murder, literally. We can't afford to do that again, look for food in houses, eh.'

'Nope.'

Max proudly opened the bulging rucksack tilting it towards Flea, she peered in nodding her head with approval.

'Any chocolate?'

Chapter Ten

The pair moved with ever more caution now. They added more effective camouflage to their clothing in the way of moss and dry grass.

They travelled slowly onwards through the open countryside for three days without incident, not speaking to each other much unless it was to warn, such as "watch out for those nettles", which in all was the most common statement they ever made to each other, maybe over a hundred times a day.

Flea suggested they should just make a little whistle through their teeth instead of that incessant old warning that was now beginning to get on both their nerves.

Before the sun rose over the horizon the two were woken by the melodic song of a lone blackbird on a branch way above them, calling to another who mimicked his call far away.

They sat and nibbled their rations with the golden pink dappled sun light steadily flickering through the foliage above.

'How's the leg?' asked Max, stretching.

'It's definitely getting better by the day.'

Flea stood up, discarded her crutch, put on her "Ghillie" jacket, pulled the rucksack onto her back grabbed her stick which up until now Max had carried and walked on. After a few paces she turned and waited for Max impatiently while he hurriedly gathered his things and followed.

Mid-morning found the two moving along the side of an overgrown hedgerow interspersed with mature gnarled oak trees every few hundred metres. On each side lay huge open grazing meadows. Ahead of them stood two large mounds perfect in shape and covered in long grass.

Max pointed ahead.

'We'll get a better view if we climb one of those small hills Flea.'

Flea turned and looked at him with disdain, shaking her head slowly.

'Did you not absorb anything during your schooling at the establishment?'

Max stopped in his tracks and held his arms out.

'What? OK they are not small hills they are humps.'

Flea whistled through her teeth and held the flat of her upturned hand towards the small hills.

'They are tumulus or putting it simply burial mounds from the late Neolithic age up until the end of the Bronze Age.'

Max's eyes lit up.

'I knew that Flea, I knew they built them in the Iron Age, I'm not daft.'

Flea prodded Max in the chest with her index finger.

'Tch, tch, everyone knows Iron Age tumulus were mostly square.'

Max raised his finger.

'Ah mostly! Those two could be Iron Age then?'

Flea turned, muttered something incoherent under her breath and carried on walking.

The two had almost reached the first tumulus when Max startled Flea. He suddenly spun on his heels and without a care in the world ran a couple of metres out into the open pointing upwards.

'I KNEW IT … I knew it! We must be close look, look Flea.'

Flea was alarmed and jumped to look to see if the coast was clear and ran out to join Max. He was watching an aeroplane banking above and heading east.

'It's over the exact spot I saw another manoeuvre only five minutes before!' He exclaimed excitedly.

'They seem to be joining a circuit right over us for an airfield Flea. It must be Cork's airfield Copham. Look, if you watch it, he's now turned again and is descending with less power look, look.'

'Get down. You'll give us away you idiot.'

She grabbed him pulling him down for better cover.

'I reckon the airfield is less than a mile or so over there.' He said flailing his pointed finger around over her head.

'I can't believe you did that. What if you had been spotted out there?'

She huffed batting his arm down.

Flea looked into Max's eyes, she realised too that they were within reach of their goal and yelped a stifled,

'Wahoo, let's get going.'

With a new spring in their step the two pressed on covering twice the distance in the same time.

That night the pair found that sleep evaded them, so they pressed on through the night and next day.

The sun an hour from setting saw them crawl to the edge of a wooded area. From this spot they could see what looked like three large olive-green aeroplane hangars behind a tree line some two hundred metres away across open land. They both agreed to hug the edge of the wooded area and cut across in the shadow of a hedgerow to the west end of the airfield.

After dark they would then cross a track to the hangars and make their way as best they could to the proposed meeting place, the airfield's windsock.

By the time they reached the track it was already dark, so making sure there were no security cameras, they stealthily crossed and made for the most westerly hangar. Keeping tight to the wooden fencing just beyond the hangar the two made their way to the edge of one of the taxiways. They dropped down flat; faces pressed to the grass. A motorcycle trundled up the track behind them its taillight moved away and disappeared out of what must have been the main gate.

The sound of traffic buzzing up and down on the busy A303 beyond the grass runway had them relying more on their sight than ears.

All was clear so the pair stood up and tiptoed out onto the grass taxiway back-to-back like two meerkats scanning the darkness.

'It's there,' Flea croaked, grabbing Max by the shoulder and spinning him around to the northwest corner of the airfield.

Around seventy metres away and silhouetted against the dim turquoise remnants of the sunset stood a windsock with its translucent sock hanging limp. Almost begrudgingly it moved around its pole as a slight breeze came and went as if to state that it was indeed a windsock.

The two stood there transfixed then broke out of their trance and without a word ran as fast as they could towards the cover of the wooden fence and made straight for the windsock.

With thirty metres to go Max pulled Flea down and pushed her into the long grass under the fence. Flea turned to Max with a look of bewilderment.

He pressed his fingers to her lips and whispered,

'Shhhh... we could be walking into a trap here. What if Cork was one of the captured?'

Flea nodded urgently and whispered, 'It's not just Cork it could be any of them. If they were captured, would they have told them the plan to meet here? I doubt it.'

She frowned and whispered, 'They wouldn't, would they?'

'You're right Flea. What if they tortured him or the others, who knows what you'd tell? I know we had exercises in mental pressure under interrogation in the complex but in reality, how would we cope and could we hold out? Don't forget we're not of service age yet.'

In the darkness Flea could just make out Max's face it had a look of total and bitter disappointment written all over it.

Reaching out and holding his arm she whispered,

'Let's find a place to hide and watch for any signs of life. If we see Cork or any of the others, we must assume all is good and make our presence known. We must, on no account go near the base of that windsock until we know for sure. Do you agree?'

Max nodded and they both retreated into the darkness.

The next morning dawned bright with not a cloud in the sky. Max and Flea had slept well. The two had returned to the wooded area and made a rough bivouac in the dark which they could use until hopefully re-united with the others.

Before dawn they had moved stealthily back up to hide in the undergrowth on the northwest corner of the airfield. They lay there camouflaged and as still as stone watching the base of the windsock with eagle eyes looking for the slightest movement.

The what ifs were constantly running through their minds.

All that toil and agony, all the risks they had taken, for what? To arrive at a place in Hampshire that may as well have been north, east or west of the research establishment. The good thing being that there was still the chance that some had reached this planned destination or were going to, like themselves. If they had overheard correctly, what those two

106

"OV" hunters had said that not one of them found had been alive. Was that good? No, it seemed selfish to think that way.

The bad side of the coin would be a trap laid for all the stragglers to fall into, metaphorically speaking of course.

A light aircraft landed on the westerly runway, slowed up and taxied off the runway taking the taxiway on the south side. Max watched it trundle away from them until it reached the mid-point of the airfield where he saw an orange flash to the right of the aeroplane almost hidden from their view by trees. He nudged Flea.

'There's another windsock! Look at the aeroplane now to the right of it, see?'

Flea nodded and muttered.

'Oh no. There is another, a third windsock. Look right over to the northeast. You have a gap in the low trees. Now look to the left of it.'

Max sighed.

'Three windsocks to keep an eye on now. Oh no.'

The two made a plan there and then. Max would move down to the middle windsock while Flea watched the nearest one. That way if there was a trap, they wouldn't both be caught. They would meet up mid-way and make a new bivouac in the hedgerow and rough ground between the south side taxiway and the A303.

If either one didn't show up after dark the other would escape. Both knew that this sounded good but would be almost impossible to do because they could not survive alone now.

Max slid off on his belly keeping low but slow, when the ground cover was good, he managed to scramble on all fours speeding up somewhat. He arrived thirty metres north of the mid-windsock at about midday but the overgrown hedgerow and tall grass that ran from his hidden position to the pole made it impossible to observe. Knowing Flea was not at his side made Max a little bolder and he pushed ever nearer. He felt confident that if he took care, he could spot the tell-tale signs of any device planted around that area.

Max stuffed extra grass into his collar and under the straps of his rucksack and then smeared more mud onto his face with his fingers making sure he was completely camouflaged. He crawled very slowly aiming to find a position several metres behind the windsock pole. That would ensure a good escape route on the roadside of the hedgerow. This spot was much better because running to the windsock and giving him a better view was a track of down-trodden grass most probably made by a hedgehog or rabbit.

As Max lay there, he glimpsed several light aircraft take off or land and taxi past. The pilots and passengers' heads were looking ahead and completely oblivious to his presence.

A couple of hours passed and Max moved closer to the base of the pole. He was within four metres and his eye caught what looked like a faint chalk mark on the very bottom of the pole. Max wriggled forward on his stomach to see what it was.

'Oh my God!' he yelped as the mark became readable.

Scrawled in chalk ten centimetres up the pole were the two letters "OV" and a tiny arrow pointing with a slight angle down to the right. Max's eyes followed the arrow's path and there half a metre away was a small pile of stones obviously arranged by hand in a square. One stone lay apart in front of the pile. Max crawled over and studied the pile. He searched excitedly around but found nothing. Then realisation hit him. He would place the lone stone on top of the square. Whoever came to check for new arrivals would then know someone had arrived. That way whoever it was, wouldn't have to make the trip every day or night as the case may be. The survivors must be some distance away.

There were six stones in the arrangement and Max wondered if that represented the day's in-between each visit or the number of survivors.

Flea had retreated back to the dense hedgerow; she was beginning to get worried about Max. He had been away for hours.

To her relief she spotted him approaching, she chuckled to herself as he was crawling like a toad at speed. He hadn't seen her and was passing a couple of metres away. Picking up a small pebble she threw it just ahead of him into the grass. Max froze dead still and thinking it could be a grass snake or adder at worst, rolled to one side and crawled directly towards her looking over his shoulder for the source of noise.

'BOO!' she barked.

Then she fell back laughing at the site of him nearly becoming airborne. Flea expected Max to give her a telling off, but no. Instead, his face lit up with glee.

'They're here, Flea… they're here. I found an "OV" sign at the base of the windsock pole. We must get back there and set up a hiding place. I think they check on a regular basis to see if there have been any arrivals.'

Flea clapped her hands together in joy.

'Fantastic, WOW!'

The two made their way back immediately.

After the sun had set and darkness fell the pair made a grass hide overlooking the hedgehog or rabbit track which

Max now realised was more likely to have been trodden down by one of the survivors.

They lay in wait trying to catch up on sleep for the first night taking it in turns to watch the track.

It was difficult enough to sleep with the excitement but when they did manage to doze off their sleep was constantly interrupted by traffic noise on the A303. This was not the ideal place to be but they had no option.

Max had followed the trodden down grass track towards the A303 the next morning but it led to a dry concrete drainage ditch and was impossible to track from there.

Who would be the survivor that found them both? Would there be two of them? Where was the camp and what was it like? What stories would they have to tell of their travels? How many of them?

Max and Flea whispered these questions to each other constantly.

As the days and nights passed the two began to become worried thinking about less optimistic questions, a plan "B".

What if the sign was made by one survivor and he or she had perished? What if the two of them were all that were left? Would they now have to find a permanent camp and take over the role of observing the windsock for new arrivals? Where would they make a permanent camp within a reasonable distance from the windsock yet safe and well hidden?

Chapter Eleven

On the fifth night Max and Flea sat at their hiding place agreeing that this constant road noise and uncertainty was going to drive them both stark raving mad. At some point soon they would have to take the decision to go for plan "B".

The decision was soon made. One more day, and then after dark they would move out and find their own place, most likely the derelict plough shed they had used.

The two agreed that they could not stand another noisy night in that place. As they turned away to look at each other and shake hands on the decision in silence they missed a small, hooded figure passing stealthily along the track towards the windsock.

On arrival at the stone arrangement the figure stepped back to observe the newly placed stone. He lifted it off the arrangement and placed it back on the ground again, then turned. He was stocky in build with a shock of dusty ginger hair sticking out from beneath a moss camouflaged "Ghillie" hooded jacket. Like Max and Flea his face was camouflaged with mud streaks. His piercing hazel eyes flashed with excitement as he blinked into the darkness. Cupping his hands together he called in a hushed voice.

'Who's there? … "OV" … anyone there?'

Max and Flea instinctively recoiled back for better cover.

Then coming to their senses both edged forward to peer along the track towards the voice.

Max couldn't reply, he just could not open his mouth. He froze there on all fours as if paralysed.

Flea rolled forward, lay on her stomach, saw the little figure crouching down and cooed.

'It's us, Flea and Max… "OV"… "OV". Who's that?'

Cork whipped his hood back to reveal his face.

'It's me, Cork.'

Cork

Max jumped up and almost trampled Flea as he ran towards Cork.

He threw himself forward and wrapped his arms around Cork giving him a huge hug.

Flea joined the two and threw her arms around them both. The trio jumped up and down together as one, their "Ghillie" jackets resembling a dancing jelly fish as they jumped in rhythm.

After their warm greetings they squatted down into the long grass looking into each other's faces in the dim light, smiling like Cheshire cats and not uttering a word. Cork raised his finger to his lips and signalled for them to follow him. Max and Flea both brimming with excitement retrieved their sticks and rucksack from the hiding place and in a line made their way to a concrete drainage ditch that ran along the north side of the busy A303.

Cork turned and with a chopped hand, signalled for them to keep stooped as they scurried westwards along the ditch.

Every now and again the headlights of a vehicle would illuminate the hedgerow alongside giving them a moment of light to see what lay ahead. Even so, all three stumbled over the odd discarded plastic bottle, a broken car wheel trim, a single old shoe to the black sparsely feathered skeletal remains of a dead crow.

Cork stopped abruptly turning so the other two bumped into him. Not having to keep his voice low because of the traffic noise he bellowed, 'Sorry about the assortment of smells along here. Won't be long now until we can cross.'

'What do you mean cross?' shouted Flea, sticking her head up and tiptoeing on her good leg to look at the cars and trucks blasting past along the dual carriageway.

Cork didn't answer and just waved them on to follow.

The ditch suddenly took on an angle down and there briefly lit by passing headlights was the opening to a culvert.

'This runs under the road. During that heavy rain a couple of weeks ago we couldn't check the windsock for two weeks because the culvert was a raging torrent of rainwater. Hope it doesn't rain in the next half an hour or we're stuffed! Come on follow me.' bellowed Cork as he slid down the concrete sump to the entrance.

The three sloshed through a couple of centimetres of dirty water with the ever-increasing disk of dim light at the other end of the pipe getting closer.

Cork turned with a flicker of a smirk on his face, his voice echoed above the sound of sloshing water and muffled rumbling traffic noise above.

'One day I'll meet a great big rat down here coming the other way, I know it.'

'Oh don't.' muttered Flea under her breath as she tried hard to keep up with them.

The three were now well into the dense woodland south of the airfield and the A303 was just a murmur of traffic in the distance.

Max called to Cork as they picked their way through the ferns and saplings.

'Such a relief to get away from that horrible road racket. How many survivors are we Cork?'

Cork, turned and seeing Flea limping plonked himself down on a fallen branch.

'Good time to rest you two.'

Max and Flea sat on either side of him. There were so many questions to exchange.

'How many survivors are with you and how long have you been at the camp, Cork?' Max blurted out enthusiastically, letting his rucksack slip from his shoulders and tumble onto the ground.

Cork looked up into the foliage as if looking for the answer.

'Er, must have been just over a month ago. Nope nearer two, I suppose.'

'What! Two months ago?' Flea asked incredulously.

Cork nodded.

'Yes, we were incredibly lucky.'

Max butted in, 'We?'

'Yes, Boo and me. He usually comes with me to check the windsock but had a dodgy tummy for the last day or two, so I had to do it alone. Well, half alone and half with you two, heh heh.'

'Wow! Good old Boo.' said Max nodding to himself.

Flea nudged Cork's knee with hers and asked in a serious tone.

'Any more survivors?'

Cork looked at the two of them in turn and replied,

'Not even half yet. We have Boo, Jin, Puk, Milo, Rob, Kat and, er, Nixi.'

Flea turned to Cork with a confused expression on her face.

'That's more than half, Cork.'

'Cork scratched his head and counted his grubby fingers.

'Hmm, yea you're right, I wasn't counting us three!'

Max chuckled and looked around.

'Where did you build the camp Cork?'

Cork waved his thumb over his shoulder.

'It's a long trek yet Max. We decided to make it a good distance from the meeting point. If it did become known to, you know who, well, the further away the better, eh.'

Cork smiled at both and after a hearty laugh said, 'You wouldn't believe how Boo and I got here in a million years. That's why we arrived first.'

He sat upright held his hands out palms upright and with a smug expression said,

'We caught the train!'

Max and Flea both asked in chorus.

'The train?'

'Yes, my little friends, the… train, as in Thomas the Tank Engine, toot-toot. It was Boo's idea. Brilliant if you ask me. When we split up outside the research centre, Boo and I headed north, yep north on foot. We attached ourselves safely to the underside of a train at Aldermaston Rail Station and after a change at Reading, arrived in Pinedever Station where we dropped down and scurried under the station platform. It was only a long trek across a few fields, and we arrived at the edge of the wood here which I must say is massive and very dense. It took longer to get from the edge of the wood to the site of our camp than the whole journey combined!'

Max turned to Flea and spoke through gritted teeth.

'Please hold him Flea while I hit him.'

The three chuckled away until Cork stood up shrugged his shoulders and peered into the darkness.

'We'll get lost if we carry on, let's settle down here and wait until dawn. Unfortunately, we won't make the evening meal!'

A plaintive voice was heard to mutter.

'Sorry, don't know what an evening meal is!'

The first rays of the morning sun found Cork leading Max and Flea through ever thickening woodland. This place was more like a rain forest than English woodland. Almost every other step had them weaving around saplings, climbing over moss-covered fallen tree trunks or ducking under large ferns. The foliage above let in very little sunlight.

The two could now clearly see why Cork had instinctively chosen this place. It was ideal. This woodland was more like a forest. Even a fox would find this undergrowth hard to penetrate.

After several hours on the go, Cork stopped and turned with a broad smile.

'Not far now, we are almost there, look.'

He pointed up to a bleached lichen-stained skull of a crow wedged between two sapling trunks.

Flea and Max looked at each other. Without a word it seemed they both had the same thought. This sign was almost pagan!

'Why the skull?' Flea asked in her best physiologist's voice.

'It's OK.' Cork chuckled, 'Don't worry. Boo found it and stuck it up there. A good thing to know you two, if anyone's away and there's any trouble at the camp, the plan is to turn it around to face the other way as a warning. We have them on all our routes to the camp, well not all animal skulls. There are drink tins, plastic bottles and so on. Stuff we've picked up near the road. Just turn the tin or bottle label to face away or whatever. We'll show you them in time.'

Half an hour later, they could see the golden sunlight illuminating what appeared to be a small clearing ahead.

Cork stopped, raised his cupped hands, placed his thumbs to his lips and blew several piercing owl hoots.

As the trio reached the clearing Cork held up his hand and stopped. He then turned and waved his arm towards the clearing as if introducing a music hall stage act and said,

'Here we are. This is our home, our new world.'

Flea and Max stepped forward and let their eyes adjust to the bright sunlight.

What greeted their eyes was somewhat disappointing, not because of the location. This place was naturally beautiful and remote. The disappointment was because there was absolutely no sign of life or any form of camp. They found themselves standing between the ferns on a low ridge overlooking a sun dappled shallow gurgling stream. The stream had an area of light-coloured sand and clay beach on either side. A steep lush moss-covered bank rose high on the other side of the stream. Beyond that, deep dense undergrowth and woodland made an impenetrable backdrop.

There was no camp, no structure and no friends to be seen. Nothing but nature.

The two gave each other a nervous glance then turned to Cork wondering if he had possibly gone mad and fantasised about the whole thing.

In utter confusion her face clouding with concern, Flea was the first to ask.

'What's here? Where's Boo and the others?'

Cork had a slightly demented grin on his face which did not help the situation.

'AHA!'

He whooped, scrambled and jumped down into water, waded across the stream and walked up the beach on the other side. Turning to the two of them, he opened his arms and did a curious whisper-shout, as if introducing a ghoulish stage act.

'It's OK to come out guys, we have Max and Flea coming to join us.'

Chapter Twelve

Max spotted movement behind the moss bank and to his and Flea's great relief, out they filed from behind the moss. The survivors, one after the other with beaming smiles. Boo, Jin, Puk, Milo, Rob, Kat and Nixi, a dishevelled little assembly. All had matted hair and looked emaciated with one or two limping. Max realised he and Flea most probably looked even more of a wreck than they did.

Boo   Jin   Puk   Milo   Rob   Kat   Nixi

Max and Flea jumped down into the water, splashed quickly through the stream and scrambled up the other side. The welcome was amazing. Max and Flea high fived, hugged and were hugged repeatedly. They held hands and all babbled away at the same time. It was a strange experience for the both of them, they had never been so close back at the establishment but now they belonged to a real close-knit family.

So many different questions, so many questions asked again and again.

Boo, slim in build with a mop of unkempt blond hair, raised his hands up and whistled to be heard,

'Come on, you two, check out your new home.'

Max and Flea followed him up the beach to the steep moss bank. Boo beckoned them to follow and walked to the place where they had all appeared. He led them, followed by the others, around and behind the moss, all became clear.

The moss was attached to netting, the netting hung down from above and was pinned with pegs at the bottom to give the appearance of a bank. Behind the false bank was a steep, one-and-a-half-metre-high irregular eroded cliff of ochre-coloured chalky clay. A narrow path led up under a slight overhang to several tunnel openings and windows that had been hewn between into the little cliff face. The dappled sunlight gave shafts of light through the moss netting making this place cool and beautiful. Flea and Max turned to each other their mouths open.

Boo beckoned them on, and they walked into the first entrance. This was a troglodyte's heaven. The two stood peering around. One passage led to another which in turn led to another. Each passage had several openings to sizable cut rooms and their hewn windows let in a reasonable amount of soft dappled daylight.

There was no sign of dampness at all. The ambient temperature was nice and cool. A light musk scent hung in the air that was quite pleasant.

Flea peered into one of the hewn-out rooms and was pleasantly surprised. The room, like the passageways was vaulted and in one corner lay a cosy bed of ferns on a tree bark base.

The inhabitant of this room had cut shelves into the chalky clay and placed their meagre personal possessions onto them. A "Ghillie" jacket and trousers hung from the wall like a scruffy green Yeti skin.

An unidentified voice came from the back of the group.

'That my room, its brill, eh?'

Flea turned to Boo who now had Cork proudly looking over his shoulder.

She held her hands, palm upwards and asked,

'How did you do all this in such a short time?'

'Well, we sort of stumbled onto it.' Cork said, folding his arms and nodding to Boo, 'We found the stream first and waded along it because it made the going easier through the thick undergrowth.'

Boo butted in.

'We didn't cut these warrens; they were here already. I think they were dug by badgers years ago, maybe when the woodland was less dense. We did however sweep them out, level the floor, cut roots back and modified them. We cut the rooms and windows of course and smoothed off the tunnel walls in places as best we could.'

Rob popped his head up behind and added, 'Its soft chalky clay, dead easy to work on apart from the tree roots we come across now and again. You could make a dance hall in this stuff within a week.'

Flea smiled and pointed up to the roof of the passage.

'Have you gone up yet or made rooms above?'

Pointing into the depths of the tunnel, shaking his head and wearing a serious expression Rob replied,

'First priority is to cut an escape tunnel out to the back. We've started but the decision is to make it really long so if this place is ever discovered we could cover a good distance underground, get out and escape. In the winter months we'll find a suitable place a reasonable distance away to the south and make an emergency hiding place that we would all aim for, if that were to happen rather than just scatter in panic.'

Flea raised her eyebrows and muttered, 'I guess then, once we reached the hiding place, we would have to do it all over again, I mean, split into pairs like before and make our way to a distant safe location to find a new home.'

Max shrugged his shoulders.

'Well, we have to think of all eventualities Flea, no matter how hard it is to chew.'

'We plan to have two inside toilets cut before the winter.' said Nixi in an exited squeaky voice, breaking the group's onsetting gloom.

Max chuckled, placed his hands behind his head and muttered,

'Cool! I am v-e-r-y, v-e-r-y impressed. You've thought of everything.'

Flea, looking more cheerful now, nodded, saying,

'Wow! Me too. Very impressive, it's just wicked.'

They all filed out chatting happily and sat by the stream in the warm dappled sunlight.

Flea turned to all of them and asked,

'What about food? What do you eat here?'

Jin, leant forward and answered instantly.

'Thank heavens for Mr Joel and our survival training. We travel a fair distance to gather all sorts of berries, nuts and even sap. We find a lot of the edible wild plants like "fat hen".

It contains more iron and protein than spinach and more vitamin B and calcium than cabbage so that's good for us. We also find a lot of edible fungi in the woods and mushrooms along the edge of the outlying fields. Obviously, we don't venture out too far.'

Milo added, 'At the moment we're trying to preserve as much food as possible for the winter months. During the autumn season we can collect acorns, grind them and rinse out the tannins, and then they can be eaten in larger quantities.'

Flea interjected.

'Max and I ate loads of "sweet Cicely" wild plant, it's so sweet and aniseed-like. Do you find it around here?'

Puk nodded.

'I collect it over on the west edge of the woods. There's lots over there. You can come with me if you like but it's hard going in that part because of the dense thicket.'

Flea clapped her hands and nodded enthusiastically.

'Yes, please Puk, I'd love to.'

Jin chuckled.

'Fortunately for us, our sudden enthusiastic thirst for knowledge on edible wild berries, fungus, roots, nuts and plants didn't set alarm bells ringing in old Jeoly's head, eh?'

Boo smiled, adding.

'Seriously, we must prepare for the onset of winter. None of us have experienced that yet, well, at least the real thing in the wild. We'll have to store plenty of food inside and try to seal the windows and doors up with discarded clear plastic bags we found in the wood along the side of the A303. For insulation we'll use bark and moss or something.

'For a test, we lit a fire the other day inside but it smoked us all out so now we plan to cut a chimney that sends the smoke into the middle of that old dead hollow tree up there.'

He thumbed over his shoulder to a big old dead hollow tree behind the Moss slope.

'The smoke can then dissipate in it on a still day you see. But until then we must troll up there, climb into that hole near the base to make the fire for our cooking.'

Suddenly, as if a bell had rung the mood changed from exuberant to serious again.

'Who's yet to arrive?' asked Max looking towards the fern covered ridge on the other side of the stream and out into the dark shadowy depths of the wood.

The direction they had arrived with Cork.

Kat shook her head. Looking down and in a whisper said, 'Ali died. She was with me. We stopped in an allotment to forage for food and take a rest when a big ginger cat attacked us. It went absolutely mad. Obviously didn't have the instinct to leave strange hairless creatures like us alone. We backed ourselves between a fence and a shed and fought it off eventually, but Ali had received a deep gash from its claws to the side of her head and neck, lost a lot of blood, got an infection and didn't recover.'

Kat sniffed and wiped tears from her eyes as Jin shuffled over on her bottom and placed her arm around her.

'I buried her in a place where her remains would never be found and laid out a bunch of daisies for her.'

Kat placed her hands over her face and sobbed.

'I would never have survived if I hadn't taken her supply of nourishment pills and I just kept going day and night in a trance.'

Flea turned and looked at Max. A tear rolled down her cheek.

Jin spoke softly, adding.

'By incredible pure luck Puk and I found Kat totally exhausted and near starvation. We found her tracks and followed them. She was not taking care about cover and we spotted her out in the open. We cared for her for a few days until she was strong enough to carry on with us. We had a scare one day. Puk was looking for berries. Kat was not right; she was still in a state of shock. I turned to find her wondering out into the open again. It was a garden and a huge black dog saw and ran towards us.

'I whacked and lunged at it with my stick screaming and yelling until the thing fled. Unfortunately, I think we were spotted by the dog's owners before I grabbed Kat and legged it.'

Flea turned to Max with wide eyes.

'We know. The big black dog was a Labrador called Toby and the big 'uns, the owners, a Mr and Mrs For… yes, Forman I think.'

Jin's mouth dropped open.

The whole group turned to Flea and in chorus asked,

'How on Earth did you know?'

Max shuffled on his backside.

'I found a local newspaper when I was looking for food. There was an article about a couple and their dog finding fairies at the bottom of their garden or something along those lines.'

The group burst into laughter. It soon petered out when they noticed Max and Flea looking serious.

Max discreetly nudged Flea's arm. They both knew all too well that Kat should have been spared the detail of the newspaper article.

'Oh, it's a long story. We'll tell you more later, not now.'

Fortunately, Nixi diverted more questions by raising her hand, as if in class and saying, in a rather callous matter of fact manner.

'Stu and I were separated, I just pressed on alone and must say at a much better pace. He was so funny. Do you remember, Stu could mimic all our tutors back at the establishment? The best one he took off though was Jeoly. If you didn't know, you'd have thought it was him. I'm really afraid for him now though. He hasn't arrived yet and I got here about two weeks ago.'

Cork changed the mood. He stood up, swept the hair away from his eyes and addressed the assembly.

'Right … We must all sit down and have meetings every three days or thereabouts to discuss task objectives and accomplishments and how we can work closely together as a team allowing each and every one of us to concentrate on activities that best match their capabilities.'

'The most important thing is a passion for our cause, and we must be optimistic about our future. There is no leader amongst us, but maybe we will have to choose one at some point.'

There was no doubt in Max's mind, Cork would be that leader. He was brilliant at it. He talked and looked like a leader. The only negative thing maybe was Cork didn't take life too seriously. OK, he had the advantage of arriving here early with lots of time to think these things out, but Max realised that he himself had not given a huge amount of thought to the future when he had had plenty of time to think, like for instance the time when Flea was recuperating with her sprained ankle.

Cork broke Max's line of thought by theatrically throwing his shoulders back. He wheeled around to face Max and Flea in military fashion and cheerily said,

'Changing the subject, we should do this exercise all the time now. We've all spent months, well some of us, crouching, creeping and very rarely have we been able to walk upright. So now we can, let's do it.'

The others nodded and let out a muted "cool".

Flea glanced at Max with a raised eyebrow, her eyes scanning his neck, shoulders and back. It was true they had both developed a stoop. Even sitting there, they had a cautious posture, ever ready to dive for cover at the sound of a snapping twig.

'He's amazing, thinks of everything,' whispered Max to Flea.

Flea leant towards Max.

'Well, don't forget we're completely exhausted and have been totally focused on getting here for months. Give it a few days and that old Max and Flea will be back again. You'll see.'

Max smiled, nodded and removed a small leaf from Flea's fringe.

Every evening after the day's labours the group would sit in a circle down by the stream for their daily meal and talk about progress in getting the camp improved, what edibles had been collected and so on.

As the evening light faded and they relaxed contented with their stomachs full, the group usually took it in turns on the subject of their adventures, getting from the establishment to the camp.

Jin would sit beside Kat to keep her spirits up. This subject was not easy for her but she generally ended up giggling or laughing along with the others at some of the exiting or bizarre tales.

On one of Max and Flea's first evenings at camp, after they had settled in the group wanted to know all about their experiences. Max and Flea regaled them with the establishment's hunter encounters, especially the rabbit hutch close call. The pylon and snake encounter and how close they came to giving up at the windsock. The rest of the group sat enthralled. Every now and again asking questions and making comparisons with their own experiences.

It seemed that all had a narrow escape with suspected "OV" hunters.

Nixi and Stu, before they became separated had almost been caught by hunters. Without a doubt the closest call. They told how they had been heading south and over the course of several nights saw the lights of a very large town ahead illuminating the night sky. The two suspected the town was Basingstoke and decided to skirt around the western edge of the town, find and follow the railway line that they knew passed Copham several kilometres to the north.

The pair set off in a south westerly direction until they intercepted the railway line. Now it was easy. Just stick to the edge of the railway line for eight kilometres or so.

Through the day the two walked along the line keeping well away from the tracks and passing trains under cover of vegetation.

During the night they made good progress, walking on top of the concrete cable ducting. Whenever they felt the vibration of a train on its way they would simply duck down behind the ducting.

They must have been spotted by night vision CCTV that had been set up by the establishment because the next night the pair stumbled through a trip wire set up over the cable ducting. There was a blinding flash. A remote camera had been set up on a rail sign and the trip wire triggered the flash and shutter. The likelihood of the camera belonging to a wildlife cameraman were remote. Who would want to take photographs of wild animals walking along cable ducting? Just in case, Stu, hurriedly scaled up the post, opened the memory card cover and yanked out the memory card. He threw it down to Nixi. She stuffed it into her rucksack and as he clambered down the post, piercing light from several torches started sweeping around along the track. They realised the hunters were onto them and seemed to be positioned on a bridge over the railway. They heard shouting and the crackle of walkie-talkies that seemed to come from all around them.

Stu and Nixi in blind panic, scampered back the way they had come, dodging the torchlight. They were trapped between the railway track and a steep embankment.

Nixi recalled that as they ran, she was aware of a loud and erratic pinging noise with dust and ballast flying up all around them.

The group unanimously agreed that it sounded like they were being shot at with silenced firearms.

Max and Flea knew that it was a dead or alive situation and so did the others in the group.

By sheer luck a passenger train came hurtling through the melee and gave them enough time to reach and duck into a large drainage pipe. The two had blundered at full speed through the pipe in total darkness until falling out into a fast-flowing stream. That's when they became separated. She managed to cling onto an overhanging branch and saw Stu swimming and floundering away into the darkness. That was the last time Nixi saw Stu.

Each one of the group told Max and Flea of their experience. But all agreed that Cork and Boo had come up with the most ingenious route to the camp. Not only that but they had found this place and then set out to find the windsock on the airfield.

One evening when Max and Flea thought all the tales had been exhausted, Milo a stocky boy with dark hair and an Asian complexion stood up, pulled up his tattered grubby T-shirt and proudly displayed a huge straight healing scar across his bare chest.

There was a light-hearted chorus from the group.

'Oh no, please spare us.'

Their story was one of the most incredible near misses.

Milo and Rob took turns in telling the story.

Milo began.

'Heading south, we had walked from sunrise to sunset. The two of us carried on until completely exhausted. It was a moonless night so we settled down to sleep in total darkness.'

Rob had a long face and was a kind looking boy.

He placed his arm around Milo's shoulders, and chipped in.

'We found a stack of old dry hay bales along the side of a field and finding a gap we climbed between two and made a nest to sleep in.

'Well, it was very comfortable, and we overslept because the next morning we were awoken absolutely terrified by something thudding sporadically into the hay bales. We clambered to the gap between the two bails and peered out to find out what was going on.'

Milo slapped his forehead.

'We had only climbed into the hay bales behind an archery range! The thudding was caused by arrows missing the targets and embedding themselves into the bails. Rob grabbed me and we both dug away desperately trying to get out through the back of the bails. In doing so, by some fluke of misfortune, an arrow about three times my height pierced the hay bale just missing Rob but skewering me though the right side of my jacket and out through the left side. Rob thought I was dead. Apparently, I was pinned while my eyes were wide open with a big saliva bubble forming on my lips like this.'

Milo blew a big saliva bubble for the benefit of the audience.

'The first thing that went through my mind was, how on earth am I going to un-pin him and hide the body?' chuckled Rob as he received a playful jab in the ribs from Milo.

'Milo suddenly burst into life, terrifying me even more. He wriggled and wriggled until he was free of his lanced "Ghillie" jacket. There was blood all over his chest. I wrenched the jacket from the shaft of the arrow and we broke through the back of the hay bales and legged it. If that arrow had been two millimetres to the left, he'd be dead now. Lucky for him the arrowhead just cut him and I think the friction of the shaft passing along the deep cut sort of cauterised the wound.'

Milo, rubbing his chest, added, 'I think it bruised a few ribs. They are better now though.'

Max and Flea found it difficult to comprehend, why the others in the camp had arrived before them. The two, honestly believed they would be one of the first pairs to arrive even with the enforced hold ups.

It appeared that in their absence and before they escaped from the establishment, the group had found and memorised as best they could, an Ordinance Survey Map found in one of the geography room cabinets. Unfortunately, Max and Flea had not seen it being committed to other duties. Because of the hurried plan to escape from the establishment the map had been overlooked.

The group were astounded that Max and Flea had arrived at the airfield at all.

In chorus the group asked Max and Flea,

'How on Earth did you know which way to head without having seen a map?'

Max gave Flea a sideways glance.

'Pylon. Remember, we climbed a pylon? Well, we had a great view from up there and could se…'

Flea broke in.

'Don't, don't, it makes me shudder even to think of it.'

This proved one thing. The training they had received back at the establishment must have been second to none.

Chapter Thirteen

Cork trekked to check the windsock at the airfield every sixth day for Stu's arrival, with either Max or Boo for company. He seemed to have a good sense with navigation through the dense undergrowth and woodland. If Cork gave Max or Boo the lead, they would invariably get lost.

As October approached the days became shorter and the weather slowly turned for the worst.

Soon the leaves would flutter gently to the damp ground and create a slippery ochre-coloured rustic carpet of textures. Even the chirping of the birds high up in the treetops would take on a different less happy note.

On a mild windy morning Puk, Max and Flea set out for the western edge of the woods to collect the wild plant "sweet Cicely".

The plan was to bring back a large bag each, full of the leaves to dry out and boil up during the winter months.

The expedition would give Max and Flea a good idea of the distance from their camp to the western edge of the wood. They set out at dawn and returned mid-afternoon two days later. This gave them both a better feeling for the camps seclusion even though the progress had been slow on their return through dense thicket laden down with their bulging bags of "sweet Cicely" leaves.

The group all agreed that before winter arrived, they should waste no time making exploratory expeditions on radial headings from the camp out to the southwest, south, southeast and east. No need to explore north because that area had been well mapped by Cork and Boo.

Max wanted to volunteer for these expeditions and looked forward to the trek east because while at the first windsock which was the highest point on the airfield, Max and Flea had spotted the lights of a service station on the rise of the A303. The service station was situated about one and a half kilometres towards the east.

Max was curious. A service station would be certainly risky to explore for supplies because of the CCTV cameras dotted around the site.

He could imagine food from the shop discarded at the back in bins, because of their being "past their sell by date".

He licked his lips. Maybe discarded out of date chocolate bars, purely for energy of course!

They certainly did not want to risk attracting the attention of the establishment to the area, but Max wanted to check it out from a safe distance to see what could be there. If the risk was too high, then maybe just collect items discarded by litter bug customers thrown into the tree line from the car park.

Jin and Kat made up a survival bag with non-perishable food, dried berries, nuts etc. and as many nourishment pills as they could spare. They wrapped it all in discarded foil and got Cork to place it under the pile of stones at the base of the windsock for the late survivor. There would be no message left with the bag just in case hostiles found it but there would be a minute cryptic clue scrawled in chalk on the windsock pole.

Their culvert under the A303 would become flooded with rainwater soon and the only way to check the windsock would be a very long hike west to go under the dual carriageway on the slip road for Pinedever Village, just too risky with little or no foliage on the trees, shrubs or ferns for cover. The hope would be that Stu, not realising the group lived in the woodland to the south on the other side of the dual carriageway would have no reason to risk a dangerous road surface crossing in desperation but would retreat to a better more secluded place towards the north and see the winter through.

Max and Flea both agreed that if it had been them arriving too late, they most probably would have gone all the way back to the old derelict plough shed and hunkered down there for the winter and then return to the airfield in the spring. The priority would have been making the place snake proof though!

The unspoken prayer amongst all at the camp would be for a mild winter to come.

While on look-out sitting camouflaged and alone up on the moss-covered bank above the camp, Max's thoughts took him right back to one of the first nights out in the open on his own.

The night he had spent up in that cosy nest high up in the small cavity on the face of that old brick wall.

He found it difficult to believe it was only months ago. For him that time seemed like years had passed.

He was more scarred now both physically and mentally.

He had aged.

On reflection Max had thought that to be captured would have meant some sort of punishment, internment and brainwashing. This organisation was very small but tremendously powerful. Now he knew that the consequences would have been extermination for them all including the younger ones and most probably some of the lesser staff at the establishment.

They would have closed ranks, tightened things up and started again after a major re-think. This time making sure that the new project "OV" developed from the embryos was a harder, more aggressive, suicidal miniature humanoid, not the free thinkers that this little band of survivors were.

Max coaxed a woodlouse away from crawling towards his leg with a twig and gazed into the shadows of the dense wood. He narrowed his eyes and whispered to himself,

'This place is not far enough away, not remote enough. I'll talk to the others tomorrow. We must think about getting as much distance as possible between us and the establishment. Maybe late spring next year when we're sure that there's no straggler to arrive, poor Stu.'

Max popped his head up as he caught site of Flea picking her way down to the stream to collect water.

She knew he was on look-out and craned her neck looking for him.

Max broke cover and waved. Flea raised her arm above her head and waved back enthusiastically. She wore the biggest smile he had ever seen, a smile that gave Max more determination than ever to do everything within his power to ensure a safe future for them all.

Chapter Fourteen

Viz   *Rip*

Miles away to the north, within the shadows of the old derelict plough shed two "OV" sized boys both stockier than Max squatted in the half-light.

A dirt-stained hand fingers outstretched gently brushed at the edge of an old footprint in the fine dust. Its owner spoke with the experience of a veteran scout.

'Yep, two of them have been here all right, no doubt about it. Maybe as long as a couple of months ago.'

The other boy nodded his head in agreement, stood up and moved away.

'I wonder who they were? There's some dry blood spattered about over there and lots of disturbed dust. Looks like some sort of struggle took place.'

Vizz's bright blue eyes narrowed as he turned and looked at Rip.

'Result. It looks like they stayed here for some time. Don't know what happened though with the dry blood and it looks like a body's been dragged outside.'

Rip let his heavy Bergen-type rucksack slip from his shoulders onto the dusty remains of Max and Flea's old bed.

He pulled at the Velcro straps and opened a waterproof plastic inner sheath.

'Give me a hand here.'

Vizz held the Bergen as Rip placed his hands on either side of a large object within, and then pulled.

Out slid a thin, compact, light-weight mobile phone.

'I hope there's a signal here. I'll give base our co-ordinates on these two fugitives tracks, well one possible fatal for their mapping.'

Almost as if hypnotised Rip straightened up robotically turned his dirt-streaked face to Vizz and snarled.

'Oh, no… give me strength… no signal here.'

Vizz slapped him on the back and plonked himself down beside the open Bergen, then spat onto the floor.

'Maybe just as well because they could zap the place to erase evidence with us in it, eh?

'Let's rest here overnight and we'll search outside for a body then move on and carry-on scouting south in the morning. Love this, simply doing what we've been trained for, eh?'

Rip was grimacing with slight discomfort.

'Don't slap me on the back again, that infernal lump of a microchip locator device they implanted in us both before we left HQ still hurts. Does yours?'

'Yea. Not surprising considering the size of the thing. Not easy to sleep either because I keep rolling onto it. Locator? Beats me what it's really for seeing as we have to update them on our location each day!'

Before sunrise the next morning, Vizz dropped Rip's boots onto a pile of sacking on the old bed.

'Come on monkey boy, get up.'

The sacking moved a little, Rip's face appeared eyes squinting.

'What's the hurry?'

'Right, I'll tell you what the hurry is mate. If we faff about every morning because of you not wanting to get up, we'll never hunt them down and complete this mission before autumn and I don't know about you, but I don't fancy the prospect of short days, rain, mud, lack of cover then frosts, sleet and snow.'

Rip pulled the sacking away, sat up and swung his legs over the side of the bed, pulled his boots on and grumbled.

'HQ did say they would get winter issue gear to us if the weather got bad but, aww, to sit down and have a proper meal instead of those terrible nourishment pills does sound appealing.'

Outside in the first light of the morning the two searched for an hour and then moved off in a southerly direction along the overgrown hedgerow. They had looked for any sign of disturbed ground where a body could have been buried but found nothing. They did however find the remains of Max's fishing dragnet stuffed under a pile of rotting timber.

Vizz and Rip instinctively followed the route that would have been chosen for good cover by the remaining fugitive

139

and, or the two if that blood had been a non-life-threatening wound.

After an hour Rip stopped and let the Bergen slip down from his back onto the ground.

'Checking for a signal Vizz. Give me a hand.'

They knelt pulled open the Velcro straps and opened the waterproof plastic inner sheath and extracted the mobile phone just enough to see the screen.

Vizz switched it on and after a moment snapped his fingers.

'Yes, got two bars. Just get the co-ordinates out of that side pocket and I'll call HQ.'

Vizz laid the paper with the scrawled co-ordinates next to the phone and punched the green button that bought up one telephone number. He punched it again, cocked his head, glanced at Rip and waited.

There was no dialling noise, just an abrupt cold answer.

'Moat … go ahead.'

'Moat, this is Victor zero, zero four how do you read over?'

'Strength five, relay your message.'

Vizz cleared his throat and in a professional radio telephony voice replied,

'Victor zero zero four, contact status Echo, evidence of fugitives found around two months old, possibly one injured at… north, five one degrees one five six one point two four. West, one four…'

As Vizz gave the rest of the co-ordinates to HQ Rip took a scaled down monocular from a side pocket in the Bergen and crawled up to an old unkempt hedgerow, then he climbed the lower branches of a sapling to scan the area.

Vizz completed the co-ordinates, then listened to a reply. He nodded looked up at Rip and winked.

'Roger, Victor zero zero four, out.'

He then pressed the red button switched off the mobile phone slid it back and secured it into the Bergen.

'Ha Moat likes us, seems like we're getting warm. What's up?'

Rip took his eye from the monocular, turned and beckoned Vizz up to join him.

Vizz pulled himself up and looked along his line of sight.

'What have you seen?'

Rip pointed across a narrow adjoining field and passed him the monocular.

'See that chestnut tree the one that's taller than the rest?'

Vizz took a long look.

'Yea, can't see anything though…'

Rip leant across and pointed.

'Check out the area in the shadow to the right of it.'

'Nope, what have you seen? Stop playing stupid games and tell me.'

Rip took the monocular and peered through it again.

'Yep, I'm not imagining it. Someone's picked up and bent a thin branch over to make an "O" and placed two small branches to look like a "V".'

Vizz grabbed the Monocular and placed it to his eye.

'Wow! You're right. You star.'

The pair loaded up and stealthily made their way around the field. It took almost two hours to reach the site. As they crept up it was obvious to see. This was no accident of nature the "O" and "V" had been stuck into the soft mossy base by hand.

If one didn't know the significance of "OV" it would be totally overlooked in passing.

As it had been Vizz's turn to carry the Bergen he squatted and watched the area while Rip crept around like a praying mantis looking for signs of life.

Rip held up his hand and looked at Vizz. He pointed to the base of a tree several metres away. Alongside the tree was a moss covered fallen hollow branch. Rip crept forward but it was impossible to be silent with the fallen leaves and mulch underfoot.

He turned and gestured to Vizz with a chopped hand towards the log then pointed with two fingers at his mouth. He turned and called in a hushed voice.

'OV... OV... anyone there?'

There was a rustle from within the hollow log then silence.

Vizz let the Bergen drop from his shoulders and moved up to the left of Rip as Rip moved forward ready to intercept a runner.

He tried again.

'O... V... we're friends, we're friends. We're on the run too. Come out, it's OK.'

A bloodied, dirt-stained face of a boy appeared at the back of the log, eyes squinting adjusting to the light, then as he tried to pull himself up, buckled and collapsed sideways with a flurry of dry leaves and lay there unconscious on his side.

Chapter Fifteen

Vizz leant over and took a long look at the boy's face.

'Yep, identified. I think this one's S-008 erm, Stu I think.'

Rip opened Stu's tattered clothing and examined his leg, swollen, deeply cut and caked in dry blood.

'Yikes, he's made a good job of that.'

Vizz fetched the Bergen and placed it beside Stu lying unconscious, pale with eyes glazed and half open.

Vizz reached into a pouch and pulled out a water canteen much to the dismay of Rip, and undoing the lid whispered,

'He's in a really bad way and well out of it. We've GOT to make sure he survives, right? This one could lead us straight to them and then… it's wipe out time!'

Vizz placed the canteen to Stu's lips and let water trickle into his mouth.

Stu coughed and gurgled, opened his eyes grabbed the canteen and desperately gulped more water. Most of it spilt over his cheeks and neck.

Vizz yanked the canteen away.

'Steady on there mate, don't overdo it. Lift his head Rip.'

Vizz held and tilted the canteen so that he could control the amount Stu drank.

'That's enough for the moment you're de-hydrated.'

Stu's eyes closed and he slipped back into unconsciousness. Rip let his head drop back and turned to Vizz.

'He's got a bad fever must be blood poisoning or something. Let's drag him back to cover behind the log we're a bit exposed here.'

The hollow log was too small for the three of them, so Rip erected a rough bivouac from twigs grass and moss while Vizz checked his pockets and possessions for any clue as to his destination.

Vizz and Rip unceremoniously dragged Stu by the hood of his "Ghillie" jacket into the bivouac and dumped him there. The two then crawled out and squatted by the base of the tree. Vizz whispered to Rip,

'He's got nothing of interest on him. No map nothing. Look, we just get this one well, get him better OK. Make him think we escaped just after them because the establishment got really hot. Tell him they clamped down and we were in fear of our lives or something.'

Rip nodded in agreement then chuckled under his breath.

'Yep OK, but he must know we were sent to special training because they were rubbish.'

Rip's eyes narrowed.

'He'll know we are after them for sure, Vizz. What then?'

Vizz gave Rip a steely look.

'If that's the case we torture info out of him and when he's told us as much as he knows, we do him in and bury him. Anyway, the state he's in, we won't know until he comes around, eh.'

Rip pointed to the Bergen laying on the ground.

'And what about that? If he does believe our story, don't you think he'll get a wee bit concerned when we say to him, 'Hang on Stu, we're just clocking in with HQ! You know force of habit and all that?'

Vizz nodded looking at the Bergen for a moment.

'I've got an idea. We report in as usual but way out of earshot of him. So, he won't get suspicious tell them the signal's bad more times than not so we don't have to call every day.'

'I don't think we tell HQ about finding S-008. You know what will happen they'll make a rendezvous with us to hand him over. Next thing you know we'll be plodding about lost in Hampshire while they extract info from him and take out the fugitives themselves. No way, we have a chance here to use him and achieve a total objective single-handed, you and me.'

'Imagine Major Rip-003 and Major Vizz-004, distinguished recognition, highly decorated, special operations and all that. We'd be well made up.'

That evening before darkness fell Rip flushed out and cleaned Stu's leg wounds. The pair knew his condition wasn't life-threatening because when he did come around, he didn't struggle, shiver or shout.

He seemed completely exhausted and the infection had tipped him into bouts of unconsciousness.

The following morning Stu woke with a start.

He appeared to have all his faculties about him. Looking around eyes wide he saw Rip and pushed himself back almost bringing down the bivouac on top of them.

Vizz ducked into the mouth of the bivouac.

'What's going on?'

Rip was kneeling restraining Stu.

'You're OK. No need to worry we're fugitives like you. We sorted you out last night and now you're better.'

Vizz crawled up and patted Stu's arm.

'No need to be alarmed look we're the same as you. Do you remember us? I'm Vizz and he's Rip.'

Stu relaxed and looked at both in turn. His mouth opened a little as if he was going to speak but nothing came out. He just looked bewildered.

Rip gave Vizz a sideways glance as if to say, "We're sussed," when Stu spoke.

'Fugitives?'

Vizz nodded enthusiastically.

'Yes, that's right, fugitives. We escaped just after you, after you escaped the establishment got really hot. They clamped down on everything, thought we were all part of the plan. They interrogated all the remaining "OVs" even the young ones. We were in fear of our lives so made a break for it one night.'

Stu nodded and raised his eyebrows.

'I'm amazed you got out knowing them. Anyway, how did you find me?'

Rip winked at Vizz.

'We were resting over on the other side of the field when I spotted the "OV" set out in thin branches on the tree-line.'

Stu rested his head back down and looked up at the ceiling of the bivouac.

'Ah I set that out hoping on the remote chance of Nixi seeing it.'

Vizz straightened up.

'Nixi? Why her? What about the others?'

Stu turned his head to Vizz.

'Why our training? We paired up into doubles. Nixi and I became separated when I ended up being washed down a stream with a great big branch impaled in my leg. Anyway, thanks for sorting my leg out you two.'

Stu looked down at his leg which was now clean and bonded with butterfly plasters. He nodded his head in appreciation.

'Where did you get the dressing from?'

Vizz shrugged his shoulders.

'Ah, we made sure we had everything we needed and loaded it all into a Bergen before we escaped.'

Stu looked confused.

'You escaped with a loaded Bergen and "Ghillie" suits? How on earth did you manage to get out with that? We could only manage to hide trekker type rucksacks with some survival equipment and "Ghillie" suits for fear the establishment would cotton on. Not only that but we couldn't get a Bergen through the culvert under the perimeter fence.'

Vizz looked at Rip as if searching for an answer.

Rip spoke up.

'Ah, which culvert did you escape through?'

Stu placed his hand on his forehead feeling his temperature.

'Um, we went to the overgrown bund wall then up and over into the wooded area on the south-eastern side and through a small culvert under the perimeter fence where we had hidden our equipment.'

Rip grinned at Vizz who was looking slightly uncomfortable at these questions.

'Ah, no. We escaped through a much larger culvert on the northeast side. Got out that way.'

Stu looked confused and turned to Rip and Vizz in turn.

'Wow, I would have thought they'd have sealed all possible escape routes by then.'

Vizz grumbled as he turned to leave the bivouac.

'Yea well they didn't, did they Rip? Oh, and thanks a lot for not giving a stuff about the ones you didn't include in your escape plans.'

Stu turned to Rip with a look of discomfort.

'Sorry about that. We didn't even know where you were. I mean we didn't have a clue you were still at the establishment. I remember you vaguely but must say we didn't dare question our tutors about your whereabouts then. Anyway, where did you go?'

Rip swept his fingers through his hair.

'We were taken to a different unit. You know another area of special operations. More to do with liaison and that sort of stuff. Anyway, better let you get some rest. You hungry?'

Stu shook his head.

'No thanks, but thanks anyway.'

Stu

Rip crawled out of the bivouac and disappeared.

Stu lay there looking up at the hap-hazard twig lining of the roof and whispered to himself,

'Weird, Fugitives. Don't think we've ever thought of ourselves as fugitives.'

He had not dared ask why they had decided to head south. No one knew other than the twelve in his group that escaped together, that the heading was to be south.

Stu stretched his good leg and peered out of the bivouac. Vizz and Rip were nowhere to be seen.

Something was wrong. The two seemed harder than the others in his group. For some reason he didn't trust them. Maybe he was far too cautious after all they had taken care of him, treated him and sorted his wound out.

Stu sighed, tutted to himself and closed his eyes.

He was being an idiot.

Before he would tell them of the Copham airfield plan he would have to ask a few subtler questions just to satisfy his doubts, and if they appeared trustworthy and as soon as he could get up and walk, the three of them would try and get to the Copham windsock and hopefully get there before autumn really set in.

On day two Stu still very weak and aching was up and hopping around with Rip's assistance. The swelling around the wound had gone down and he could bend his leg slightly now.

He had not had much opportunity to talk with the other two in depth. They had appeared to be frustrated to the point of being rude at the hold up, so much so that Stu felt obliged to get up and about before he felt fit and ready.

He chose to ask Rip in the absence of Vizz.

'Where are you two heading for? I mean what's your plan?'

Rip, turned to Stu and shrugged his shoulders.

'We have no real plan. Just get as far from H... I mean base ... the establishment as possible. What about you? What's the plan?'

Stu pretended to stagger playing for time to think. Rip grabbed his arm and sat him down on the ground.

Stu had remembered a site Mr Joel had mentioned a few times back at the establishment.

The group were to have a one-week survival training exercise there. The place was chosen because most of the area was prohibited access to the public. Playing for time he waved his arm to the west.

'I really don't know the exact location Rip. We had a plan to all meet up in a wooded area at the Lintebourne Military Range.'

Rip whistled through his teeth as he glanced around for Vizz.

'Ha, we had survival training there last January. Good choice, very clever but not exactly right to stay in that place for too long with soldiers on exercise there now and again.'

Stu was taken aback that Rip and Vizz already had survival training at Lintebourne, after all they were the same age as the others. Why had they been chosen? Stu looked up at Rip and shrugged his shoulders.

'Well, the idea was to get as far away from the establishment meet up and then make plans to carry on and find a better place to hide.'

Rip knelt beside Stu.

'Sit here I'm off to find Vizz.'

Stu watched Rip slope off and disappear into the undergrowth. He was even more suspicious now. They never called the establishment the "establishment" but called it base. Not only that but he swore that Rip almost slipped up and called it "HQ" at one point.

Still feeling weary, it was difficult to comprehend exactly what was happening.

Something was wrong with those two. Why had they had more advanced training and why had they been taken out of the group all that time ago?

The odd thing was, if they were hostiles, connected to the establishment they would have tried to hand me over by now for interrogation. Surely, they would have dragged me to a known meeting place to hand over to the "OV" hunters.

Stu knew it would be impossible for him to escape these two if he had to. He wouldn't get far before they caught him in his state. He also knew that they seemed to be better trained to the point of excellence.

He would have to play along for as long as possible.

If they had escaped and he seriously hoped they had and meant well, then he would change course and try to find the airfield at Copham. If he was still suspicious, he would think of something to tell them, some reason why the destination was Winterbourne.

He would have to survive with them and give up hope of finding the others for their sake.

Vizz and Rip returned with Vizz carrying the huge "Bergen" rucksack. He placed it behind the bivouac and walked over to Stu. There was an intimidating air to his voice.

'So, I hear your trying to get to the Lintebourne Military Range to meet the rest of the fugitives? We had training there but I'm not sure exactly where it is. I know it took a hell of a long time to get there by road. We couldn't see a thing because we were in the back of a security van. You must have some idea?'

Stu tried his best to look unfazed.

'I know its southwest and we have a long way to go. We planned to head to the military airfield Boscombe Down. We would then hopefully see military traffic flying in and out. The plan was then to head south or southwest and try and find the place.

Vizz shook his head and folded his arms.

'You must be all mad. It has to be at least fifty kilometres from here. Walking at our size will take us into next year.'

Stu shrugged his shoulders and looked up at the two of them.

'Well, that was the plan an…'

He was cut short by Rip.

'Is there some way of getting there other than walking? Look if we hitched a ride under a car or truck or something we could get down there, maybe before the others. Can you imagine? We could have a nice reception party for them as they roll in, heh heh.'

Vizz stroked his chin and nodded.

'Yea I see where you're coming from Rip but hell, it would be risky.'

Rip held his hands out palm up.

'Well fancy spending winter trudging day in day out up to your armpits in rainwater and with frost or snow not being able to move just in case our footprints gave us away? No way.'

Vizz strode over to the bivouac and kicked it down scattering the twigs and moss around until it was all part of nature then picked up the "Bergen" and swung it onto his back.

'Right, we'd better get a move on then and find your mates.'

Stu hobbled along, his leg throbbing painfully with each stride. Vizz lead the way with Rip following up in the rear.

That evening they settled down on a pile of dry leaves under a thick hedgerow.

Vizz made some excuse to wonder off. He took the "Bergen" and disappeared.

Rip lay on his side, pulled the hood of his jacket over his face and within seconds fell sound asleep his breathing changing to a steady snore.

Stu, pulled himself up and crept away in the direction that Vizz had disappeared.

In the half light and silhouetted by the lights of what looked like a service station several hundred metres away, he spotted Vizz, kneeling over something that appeared to be emitting a dimmed green glow.

Over the sound of the distant road traffic, Stu heard Vizz talking.

'… zero four. Tomorrow turning onto a westerly heading. No contact this time but have found evidence of fugitives, maybe three weeks old and making progress tracking them. Over.'

There was a pause as Vizz appeared to be listening, then he spoke again.

'Roger Victor zero, zero four out.'

Stu was dumfounded, he crept stealthily back to the hedgerow as quickly as his bad leg would allow him and lay down near Rip.

Vizz returned carrying the "Bergen" and settled down to sleep.

Stu's mind was in turmoil as he lay there.

Tracking them, tracking them. The words ran in a loop through his mind repeatedly.

His suspicion was confirmed. What an idiot he was, it was patently obvious Vizz and Rip were hunters. They were using him to track down the others.

At first light the trio stirred. Stu had hardly slept a wink all night. He had rolled around thinking trying to formulate a plan but found it almost impossible to concentrate. His instinct was to escape but he knew that the further he led the two away from the area the safer the group would be, well and the fact that with his leg, and their tracking skills they would catch him and know he was aware of their motives.

He had to play along.

Vizz stood up, stretched and winced in pain.

'This micro-blasted chip. How's yours?'

He turned to Rip.

Rip grumbled.

'I have to sleep on my left side because of it and the "Bergen" doesn't help. Lugging it day in day out.'

Vizz looked down his cold steely eyes fixed on Stu.

'And what about you? Suppose your gammy legs taken the pain away from your chip, eh?'

Stu looked up at both and in a rather apologetic voice replied,

'I haven't been fitted with one yet.'

Vizz cried out.

'WHAT? You and all the fugitives haven't got one? Ah, it all makes sense now. That's why they couldn't locate them Rip.'

Realising he had slipped up Vizz quickly changed track.

'Yeh, well we escaped before they activated our locators, didn't we, Rip?'

Stu looked at both in turn.

Locators like transponders?

They didn't have a clue.

Should he try and tell them that the devices implanted into their bodies could be triggered to explode vaporise them and eliminate everything within several yards around them?

Should he tell them for that very reason the group had escaped into the outside world?

Why, if they didn't know about the true purpose of the device did they need to escape? If he told them and they called "HQ", would "HQ" terminate them there and then or fob them off and make him look like a liar?

Either way he would lose his life. Go up in a puff of smoke or be angrily bludgeoned to death by them and his remains handed over to their "HQ" as a so-called fugitive that resisted capture.

Stu didn't have to make the decision there and then because Rip kicked his good leg and barked, 'You going to sit there all day then?'

As Stu struggled to get up ignored by the other two, Vizz told Rip about the service station he had spotted the previous night.

The three made their way along the hedgerow and crawled out into a field.

Vizz pointed to a green and yellow sign just visible above the tree line several hundred metres away.

'That's where were going to catch our ride. Only trouble is it looks like there's a damn great dual carriageway to cross to get a lift in the right direction.'

Rip pulled out the monocular and studied the line of trees that bordered the dual carriageway.

'Heh, heh. Got it. Looks like there's a way across.'

He handed the monocular to Vizz.

'Look over there where the road rises. There's like a big tube or arch in the embankment for a stream maybe.'

A police car heading east with its siren blaring and blue flashing lights caught their attention.

'Look, look see the police car whizzing along there? It's going over it right… now.'

'Your right mate, got it.'

With that they crawled to better cover and headed towards the embankment.

An hour later they heard the buzz of an engine approaching. A tiny aircraft, a microlight flew low right over their heads sending them sprawling for cover. It appeared to be approaching an airfield to the west for a landing.

Stu gasped craning his neck to watch it disappear behind the treetops. Without a doubt they had almost stumbled upon "Copham".

Vizz and Rip got up grabbed him by the shoulder and carried on.

From the soles of his feet to the top of his head, Stu was filled with a crushing hopelessness.

Just an airfield to them, they didn't have a clue how this experience had hit him. He was so close but yet so far from ever seeing his friends again.

Everything he had dreamt of over the past months was about to slip away. He had to lead them as far away from this place as possible.

Chapter Sixteen

Just over two weeks had passed since Max had volunteered to explore the boundary of the wood.

Cork liked the idea of checking out the service station to the east but on the proviso that they kept to a safe distance and would not compromise themselves.

The plan was made. Cork, Max and Flea would head out that way then head west along the southern edge of the A303 until they reached the culvert. They would then, depending on the depth of rainwater in the culvert go under the A303 to check out the windsock on the airfield.

Two days later just after dawn and with enough light to see where they were going the trio set off with their rucksacks loaded with food and water.

The dense damp undergrowth made for heavy going into unexplored territory.

By midday they came to a rutted earth track running from south to north. The track looked rarely used as long grass and ferns grew between the deep ruts left by the tyres. Max, keeping stooped low, checked all was clear and crept out to examine the tyre tracks.

'It looks something like a Land Rover and trailer I think.'

He rubbed his fingers over the earth and turned to the other two keeping low as they peered over a clump of grass.

'This track hasn't been used for a while, there's weed's right here in the indentation of the tracks.'

Cork and Flea joined him, looking left and right just in case.

Flea gave Cork and Max a frown.

'That's not good. I thought we would have to travel some way from camp before we came across a track.'

Max nodded, turned and took a long look up the track to the south and north.

'I don't know the reason for this track. Maybe it's just for a farmer collecting logs in the winter months. I'm sure there's no need to worry. I would doubt very much anyone the size of a farmer or lost rambler would battle their way through what we've come through and anyway if they did, we would hear them coming half an hour before they got to us at camp, eh?'

Cork jerked his thumb over his shoulder.

'With the camouflage moss netting they would pass the camp and not even know it was there.'

They all nodded in agreement and moved on eastwards.

This would not be the only track they found.

In total they had to cross five tracks that criss-crossed the woodland. Unfortunately for them none ran in an easterly direction.

During the morning of the second day and as the trio weaved through the dense undergrowth a strange banshee-like wailing noise made them dodge down for cover and peer with wide eyes into each other's faces.

'What the hell's that?'

whispered Flea.

The noise passed and seemed to head off in an easterly direction.

Cork raised his head and chuckled.

'It's a siren, ambulance or police car on the A303.'

'Wow didn't it sound spooky through the trees?'

Somewhat relieved they moved on.

Towards the end of the day the noise of distant traffic became louder with every twist and turn of the undergrowth.

With their acute sense of smell the whiff of fumes, coffee and fried food from the service stations forecourt became ever stronger.

They decided to settle down for the night and press on early in the morning rather than get too close and have a sleepless night with the traffic noise and smell.

The trio made a hasty bivouac, ate some of their rations and settled down.

All three were physically exhausted but they lay there in the darkness finding it hard to sleep.

Max turned his head to listen.

'Does this remind you off our waiting near the windsock Flea? That constant traffic noise,'

Flea muttered.

'Yea, but it's further away here so not too bad, eh?'

She turned to the dark shadow that was Cork's head.

'Do you think Stu may have drowned in that river? If he didn't, I can't bear to think off him alone, arriving at the windsock and having to turn away because nobody turned up. It wouldn't be so bad if you had a partner to plan things out with. To be on your own and not be sure if anyone would turn up there would be a killer.'

Cork sniffed and turned to Flea.

'Look, we'll only stay there until night falls then we'll check the place out and head west along the edge of the A303. It certainly won't take as long as it took getting here. We'll be there on the fifth day check, you'll see. Just hope the culverts not flooded, that's all.'

With that he rolled over and let out a huge sigh.

'Come on, we'd better get some sleep it's going to be a long day tomorrow and we're going to need all our strength. Night Flea, night Max.'

At the first hint of light the next morning the chorus of bird song woke them.

By the afternoon the trio were close enough to see the service station through the trees, beyond the petrol pumps a "Burger Chef" restaurant.

They had arrived at the rear of the complex and could clearly see a timber lattice fence enclosure with wheelie-bins, gas cylinders and rubbish bags behind.

As far as they could see there was no CCTV cameras in this area but quite a few covering the fuel pumps and exterior of the Burger Chef.

The plan was, under the cover of darkness one of them would investigate the enclosure.

Crawling stealthily on they arrived in the undergrowth behind the shop car park adjacent to the petrol pumps.

The only litter discarded by people in the car park was not worth a second glance.

Max chuckled to himself, turned to the other two and with both hands pretended to lick them and brush his face and head.

Flea looked confused.

'Keep down. What on earth are you doing?' she whispered.

'I just feel like a rat, Flea!'

They all giggled.

Cork tilted his head, listening to the rumble of distant thunder. He held a finger to his lips.

'Shhhh... It looks like rain. Let's move back to that fence enclosure and sit it out there until dark.'

Chapter Seventeen

As the light faded, a vehicle-transporter truck drove into the truck parking area. The dazzling beam from the headlights revealed a fine drizzle.

Fully laden with shiny new cars it pulled up between the trio and the fence enclosure. With a loud hiss and wheeze the hydraulic brakes were applied and lights turned off.

They watched as a pair of overall-clad legs dropped down on the other side of the cab, the heavy work boots splashing in a puddle. Mirrored in the wet asphalt the driver stomped off in the direction of the Burger Chef.

'Great. Let's hope he has a huge supper. That truck will give cover on the way to that enclosure. Who's going?'

Max volunteered without hesitation.

Flea placed her hand on his shoulder and whispered in his ear.

'Don't take any risks. It's not worth it for scraps. Not even for out-of-date chocolate or bread!'

Max nodded, smiled and was just about to move forward when Cork grabbed both by the arm and pulled them down with urgent force.

He looked like he'd seen a ghost.

'Shhhh… jeez… I don't believe it. Don't move.'

Flea glanced at his line of sight and followed it but could see nothing through the overgrown foreground.

'What? What have you seen?' gasped Max.

Cork slowly crouched down and turned to them.

'I'm absolutely convinced I saw a figure, maybe two in the shadows over there by the enclosure. I mean "OVs", us, not biguns.'

Flea gasped in excitement.

'We have to signal to them. Max, quick it could be Stu and... who would the other one be?'

Max raised his finger to his lips.

'Yes, exactly. Who could the other one be? We must stay cautious. This could be a trap, remember.'

Cork crawled forward to get a better view flanked by Max and Flea.

After what seemed an age a distant flash of lightning revealed a small figure appearing from behind one of the wheelie-bins and too far away to be identified. He looked to make sure the coast was clear then reached back and grabbed another.

The trio watched as he pulled. The second figure seemed to shamble forward then trip and fall onto his knees.

Flea gasped as a third crouched figure appeared, took the kneeling one by the scruff of his collar and then dragged him unceremoniously towards the rear of the truck car trailer.

'Who are they? Look at the middle one. He looks like he's wounded and in trouble,'

whispered Max.

On reaching the shadowed nearside rear of the trailer the first character jumped up, grabbed the car ramp then pulled himself up, he reached down and grabbed the second by the wrists while the third lifted him up by his legs.

Stu let out a stifled yelp as Vizz wrapped his arms around his legs and lifted him. A searing pain wracked through his injured leg. He tried to push Vizz away but Rip had grabbed his wrists and was pulling up with all his might.

As quick as a flash Stu was hauled over to the side strip of the wet chequer plate ramp and rolled over clutching his leg in agony. Tears of pain rolled down his cheeks.

Vizz passed up the Bergen and without hesitation followed it onto the ramp.

Without a word Vizz passed Rip and hauled Stu up the incline of the ramp to the wheel of the first vehicle while Rip took hold and dragged the Bergen up behind.

Vizz scanned the underside of the car for a likely place to hide for the journey.

He then hissed, 'There's nowhere for three of us to hide under this one, it's too compact.'

Rip looked up and down the row of cars.

'We'll have to climb up behind a wheel each, under the wheel-well. You take the first one Vizz, I'll take the front wheel-well and you, get up there to the second car and hide.'

He shoved Stu in the back. Before Stu crawled away Vizz barked at both.

'Remember, this thing's heading west so I'll check road signs on the way and if I see anything that's close to our destination I'll come up and get you two. We'll wait for the truck to stop, traffic lights, roundabout or whatever and get off. That hinged ramp at the back should hide us from following traffic, OK?'

They both nodded and took their positions.

As Stu painfully pulled himself up behind the rear wheel of the second car he glanced back and noticed Rip securing the Bergen under the tyre of his wheel before pulling himself up under cover of his wheel arch.

Stu perched himself on the rear axle of his car. He sat with his back to the wheel and passed his right arm through the brake hose to secure himself.

This was going to be a very uncomfortable damp, cold, and draughty ride but at least he didn't have to stagger through the wet undergrowth on his injured leg at their legionnaires pace.

Stu sat there, the odd flash of lightning, dimly illuminating his surroundings, the shiny new pipes, hydraulic arm and under-seal. He took a breath and noticed the smell of a new car overpowering the odder of his damp and blood encrusted clothes.

In preparation for the ride, Stu hunched forward, placed his chin on his chest and pulled the hood of his jacket over his head in an attempt to shield the damp draft while he waited. He could imagine the madness that would ensue when Vizz decided to abandon the truck. Traffic lights, roundabout! To drop down with that big Bergen unseen by following traffic would be difficult enough, let alone running across a pavement or grass verge to hide.

Anyway, he really did not care if they were spotted. As long as the three of them were seen and reported a good distance from here was all that mattered right now.

Stu's line of thought was interrupted. Was it Vizz or Rip reaching up shaking his foot? He grumbled to himself, 'What now? Please, please don't make it a change of plan.'

He wearily pulled his hood back and looking down in the half-light and saw the silhouette of one of them.

'What? What is it now?'

'Shhhh… Hey, is that you, Stu?' came a kinder, slightly familiar voice.

Stu pulled his hood right back, eyes wide open, not quite believing what he was hearing.

'Who... who's that?'

'It's me, Max. Look, don't make a sound. Who are the other two? Can I go and get them?'

Stu grasped Max's hand tightly and pitched forward, urgently whispering over a long rumble of thunder.

'Max, it's really you? I can't believe it. NO... NO... they're hunters. Do you remember Vizz and Rip? Well, they're establishment hunters. I led them to believe we were gathering in the Lintebourne Military Range. It's some distance west of here. That's why we're on this truck. The plan is to use me to find you all and then they'll eliminate the lot of us.'

Max glanced over his shoulder and in a flash, ducked behind the wheel of the car, popping up on the other side just in case he was spotted by the other two.

'What? You mean Vizz and Rip who disap...'

Stu cut Max off.

'Hey, look, there is no doubt, they plan to kill us all and I mean all.'

'I've got a plan. You must hide further up the ramp now, just in case, and as soon as this truck starts up, help me down from here, I've got a gammy leg and can't move very well. There's a Bergen stuffed under the front wheel of the last car. It's important you grab it, careful though. Whatever you do don't let them see you, because Rip is above on that axle.

'Go along the edge of the ramp, you'll be hidden by the wheel.

'As the truck starts to pull away, we have to jump for it with that Bergen. OK?'

Max saw the look of relief and elation on the tear-stained, grime masked face of Stu and knew he had to do this.

As he moved up to hide behind the rear wheel of the third car on the ramp, he motioned to Cork and Flea with his hand held up vertically and out flat to stay hidden.

Cork turned to Flea and shrugged his shoulders.

The two had seen everything but were completely confused.

'What does he want us to do?' whispered Flea looking enquiringly into Cork's eyes.

'I don't know. I'm sure he wants us to stay hidden for some reason.'

Flea could not understand why he had only approached the first of the hidden three. Something was wrong.

She lifted herself up on all fours and was about to sprint to the trailer where Max had hidden when Cork grabbed her leg and pulled her back down.

'Too late, Flea. Get down, look the driver is coming back.'

'What on earth are they doing?' she gasped as she dropped back down onto her stomach.

The cab door of the truck slammed shut behind the driver. Vizz dropped down from his hiding place. He ran crouched along the ramp to Rip and Stu in turn.

'You, good?'

Rip leant over and gave a thumbs up.

Vizz moved along to Stu.

'Oi you, good? Come on, are you OK?'

Stu leant over and gave a thumbs up.

Vizz muttering under his breath hurriedly returned to his hiding position above the front steering assembly of the first car.

A couple of minutes passed and then the truck engine coughed into life, the vibration sending a cascade of cold rainwater falling from the cars.

Max crawled out from behind his wheel on all fours and scrambled to Stu who was already lowering himself down. Max, dazzled by the brightness of the truck's red rear lights, grabbed Stu's jacket and swung him around, then indicated he should move up the ramp and away from the other two.

Stu opened his mouth to say something but the loud hiss and wheeze of the hydraulic brakes releasing drowned out his words.

The truck started to move forward almost sending Max headfirst over the edge of the ramp.

Being careful to stay hidden behind Rip's car wheel he crept along and took hold of the Bergen.

The movement, noise, flash of huge brake lights and lightning helped to cover Max and distract Rip and Vizz.

Max dragged the heavy Bergen away up the trailer ramp towards Stu who was crouched by the front of the third car and frantically beckoning him to hurry up.

Cork and Flea watched in terror as the truck crept away slowly gathering speed. They could see through the shroud of drizzle and spray from the tyres two silhouetted figures hanging down clinging onto the inside edge of the car ramp, then they let go together.

The two dropped with some sort of sack from at least one and a half metres to the wet asphalt.

The huge nearside quadruple wheels of the truck's trailer rolled towards them as they lay crumpled and winded.

Flea grabbed Cork's arm tight and let out a helpless scream which was drowned out by the rev and crunching gear change of the huge machine.

Max, stunned by the heavy landing gathered his senses and his adrenaline kicked in.

In an instant the two pushed themselves up onto hands and knees, saw the great tyres rolling towards them and threw themselves to the left. As Cork and Flea were about to give a sigh of relief, they saw one of the pair lunge towards the big sack, grab it and yank the thing away with a fraction of a second to spare before it was crushed by the tyres.

At that moment the pair were hidden from view as the huge tyres rolled past.

The car trailer moved over them and the truck accelerated away in a cloud of swirling drizzle.

The two could have been easily mistaken for a bundle of old rags huddled with the sack on the wet asphalt.

With indicators flashing, giving an orange strobe effect to the side of the building the truck rounded a corner and entered a slip road, disappearing from view with the whine of its engine and hiss of its tyres on the wet asphalt fading into the distance.

Cork and Flea knelt side by side then turned to each other mouths open as the bundle of old rags stood up and staggered towards them. One had an arm around the shoulder of the other, hopping ungainly while dragging the big sack.

The two eventually reached the spot where Cork and Flea had remained hidden, they crashed through the undergrowth and almost fell in a heap on top of them.

Max, panting and puffing looked up at Flea. He turned and pulled the hood from Stu's head.

Cork and Flea focused on the face and in unison gasped.

'God! It's Stu.'

Stu sat up, nodded to them each in turn, a huge white toothy smile spread across his mud-caked face.

Flea knelt beside him, placed her arm around his shoulder and gave him a hug while Cork rolled the Bergen off his legs.

Stu, in between catching his breath whispered,

'Aww, man, man, man, can't believe this? I've found you. No, you found me, oh I don't know!'

The smile morphed into a look of pain. He groaned and looked at Max.

'I think my wound has split open. Would you have a look in the side pocket of the Bergen, I think there's some dressing, butterfly plasters or something.'

Flea looked towards the slip road where the truck had disappeared, turned to Max scrutinising his face and fired a string of questions.

'Oh, God. Those other two are still on that truck? Why didn't they get off with you two? Who on earth were they Max? It looked like you were hiding from them on that trailer from where we were. Why, where they "OVs"?'

Stu held up his hands and interrupted her.

'Those two were Rip and Vizz, remember them?'

Flea let out a gasp and shot a glance at Max, she was taken aback by the answer.

'Well, they're establishment hunters, real nasty killers. Their mission is to track us all down and eliminate us. They're good, I mean really good at their job, and somehow they've been completely brainwashed. They found me sometime after I was separated from Nixi. I was really sick, blood poisoning or something with this leg and, oh it's a long story. Anyway, they were using me to lead them to the rest of you, but I overheard Vizz updating HQ on that thing.'

He looked over to the Bergen and asked Cork to search it while Max and Flea attended to his wound.

Cork pulled at the Velcro straps and opened the waterproof plastic inner sheath. Stu placed his hands either side of a large object within and then pulled. Out slid the thin, compact, light-weight mobile phone.

Max, Flea and Cork leant forward staring incredulously, mouths open.

'A mobile coms device. Does it work?' whispered Flea, pulling the plastic sheath down to reveal the buttons.

Stu reached out and lifted her hand away.

'Whatever you do, don't activate it. It works, OK, and this is what those two used to report to HQ, the establishment.'

'Hey, hang on a minute Stu,' Cork asked looking towards the slip road.

'What happens when they reach wherever it was you were going, find you and this thing is missing? They'll come back here and track us all down.'

Stu looked at the three in turn.

'After I realised that their plan was to exterminate us, the fugitives, I fed them a story. I made them believe we planned to meet up somewhere within the Lintebourne Military Range. It's some distance west of here. You remember, we were going to have some sort of training exercise there in the future? That's why we climbed onto that truck. They had no idea that I knew their plan, so as far as they were concerned, no reason to escape.'

Max shook his head and frowned.

'OK, I know that's noble of you Stu and we have their phone their means of communication with the establishment but what happens in a month or so when they've somehow made contact with their HQ and the last place they saw you was here, less than a few kilometres from our camp?'

Stu wiped his mouth with the back of his hand then reached over and patted the phone.

'That's where this little fella's going to come in useful, but we'll have to stick around here for a couple of hours.'

Chapter Eighteen

Drizzle flecked onto the windscreen of the car transporter highlighted with the odd flash of lightning. The blades of the windscreen wipers swung rhythmically back and forth over the glass, pushing greasy water from its surface.

That sausage, mash, eggs and beans followed by treacle tart and ice cream had done the trick, but the coffee was wearing off. He was feeling drowsy, after all it was a couple of hours ago he had drunk it.

The driver opened his cab window ajar and let cold damp air waft his cheek.

He checked his rear-view door mirror. Yes, it was still there, even though he had maintained a steady sixty miles per hour and those headlights were glued to his rear.

The vehicle had been locked onto his tail for at least forty-five minutes along stretches of dual-carriageways, A-roads and bye-passes around the odd town and it was still there when he left the A303 and travelling down the A338 on his way to Salisbury. He was hoping to get to Weymouth by early morning. The plan was to arrive and unload his cargo of shiny new Mitsubishi compact crossover 4x4s to the dealer's showroom before they opened to customers at eight-thirty that morning.

As the truck approached the town of Porton the driver's attention was again drawn to his door mirror.

The tailgating vehicle had pulled out and it sped alongside the trailer. It was a large Mercedes 4x4. After overtaking it cut in front of the truck with blue-flashing lights in the rear window and with the dibbing of brake lights had the truck driver braking to a halt.

Two men in Barbour style coats climbed out of the 4x4. One trotted over to the driver's side of the truck cab and waved what looked like a police type badge in a folder up at him as the other man made directly to the rear with a torch.

The driver opened his window, stuck his elbow out and bellowed, 'What's goin' on, mate? What's the matter?'

The man climbed up to the cab door and flipped the badge open in the light of his cab.

'UKBA. You'll know us as the UK Border Agency. We had a report from a driver following your vehicle that he saw, what he thought could be someone hiding under the chassis. We'll just do a quick investigation. It's all to do with suspected illegal immigrants coming into Britain from the ports and heading for the west country.'

The truck driver slapped his forehead and laughed.

'Phew, that's a relief. I was watchin' you back there for miles following me finking you were goin' to hi-jack my cargo or sumthin.'

The agent patted his elbow and chuckled.

'No need to get out sir, its filthy weather out here. We'll just do a quick check and send you on your way. Like most of these alerts, it'll be nothing. Just someone you cut up getting his own back I wouldn't doubt.'

The truck driver sneered as he reached forward for his roll-up pouch.

'Ha, don't tell me, road users these days, eh.'

Five minutes later the agent came back to the cab.

'Thank you, sir, we've checked the vehicle out and all seems good. I'm terribly sorry for the delay but as you can imagine, we have to check out every single report.'

As the truck pulled away and headed off to its destination the 4x4 reversed up the road to the agent with the torch.

He opened the back door and let in what could have easily been mistaken for two small wet terriers.

The 4x4 drove off at a steady speed.

Two small heads, dimly lit by the 4x4s instrument panel appeared between the front seats.

Vizz spoke first.

'Sir, Sierra-zero, zero, eight was with us. He must have fallen or something.'

The driver glanced over his shoulder and barked.

'You have a lot of explaining to do. First, you two make contact with a fugitive and do not report it. Secondly you lose him and your mobile coms which is unique to our organisation. I only hope both the phone and he fell and were run over by a truck so that their remains would be obliterated.

'Thirdly, you take an incredible risk by jumping onto a truck and hitching a ride like it was a number thirty-five bus!'

The second man snarled at Vizz and Rip.

'We have been following your every move from a distance. The locator chips that you had inserted into your bodies tells us, to within three metres your position and that's anywhere in the world, get it?

'So, imagine our surprise when your signal starts heading up the A303 at sixty miles an hour! I want to know why and NO bull?'

Vizz and Rip told them everything in detail and took great efforts to edit out the fact that they wanted to make the kill themselves.

The driver spoke in a sickly intimate voice.

'We're just a few miles from Lintebourne. We'll supply you with another mobile com, and don't lose it, OK.

'You will stay and greet the fugitives as they arrive. When I say greet, I mean gather them, interrogate and dispatch them, oh, and keep the bodies for us to collect later.

'You will both stay at this planed meeting location for however long it takes them to come in in their dribs and drabs.

'You must extract as much information from each fugitive before terminating them. If any remain unaccounted for, I want to know, what they think and how they think so that we can predict their strategy and hunt down, every single one of them.'

The second man, waiting for a rumble of thunder to abate, piped up.

'We've been incredibly lucky so far. All sightings have been seen by the media as being the usual copycat nutter trying to get attention for themselves or we've dealt with CCTV evidence just in time.

'That means you two have to be extra vigilant. No more of those stupid wild ideas like that last episode. You report daily now, no excuses.'

Vizz and Rip acknowledged in unison.

The driver turned away and prodded the keyboard on his mobile phone.

'Sasquatch? Yep, this is Davis. We may have a roadkill and a coms set that needs immediate attention. Yep, I'll fill you in later, haven't got time now.

'You need to scan the nearside lane westbound from Copham services on the A303. Turn off on the A338 until Porton. If you find no remains between those points, I want you to turn around and search again until you do find something. It's not going to be easy in these conditions.

'Now, if Sierra zero, zero, eight is a shovel job I'll be happy. My fear is that he'll be recognisable. You know, you've seen it many times I bet, the fox with the flat body and complete head God forbid.

'OK, report any finding immediately to me.'

The driver dropped the mobile phone into the centre console of the vehicle and started the engine.

The two men agreed to drop Vizz and Rip off on the northeast side of the Lintebourne range. The most likely place for arrivals to appear.

Vizz asked the driver who seemed to be the higher ranking of the two men if they could drop them off at dawn. That way the awful weather would have passed and they wouldn't have to set up a bivouac for the remainder of the night.

Mr Davis almost spat with anger.

'You, little rats. Do you seriously think we're a taxi service? I'll drive you as far into the range as I think suitable and you two will jump out and do YOUR DUTY. GOT IT?'

Almost as if on cue, there was a loud clap of thunder as he turned away muttering to the windscreen.

The second man threw a packet of chocolate buttons onto the back seat.

'Here, get your sugar levels up.'

Vizz and Rip grabbed and tore at the pack ejecting most of the contents over the seat. They both scrambled and gorged on the chocolate buttons.

The driver threw a glance over his shoulder and scowled.

'Don't tell me you've lost your rations as well? Flippin amazing! And they say you lot are the "OV" elite. God, help us.'

Rip glanced up with hate in his eyes but soon realised that he was losing out on the frantic chocolate button gathering feast.

Chapter Nineteen

Max reached over and pulled the edge of the old plastic bag down to let the rainwater shed off. It had kept the small group camouflaged, dry and cosy while Stu recounted his exploits with Vizz and Rip.

Max shook the cold rainwater from his hand and turned to the others.

'So, I think we're all aware now that Vizz and Rip will return here at some point and track us down to our camp or get the establishment to do an aerial survey of the woodland, find the camp and blitz us in one hit. We have to strike camp ASAP and get the hell out of the area.'

Stu shook his head and pulled himself up onto his elbow.

'I hate to do this. It feels wrong but I have to do it for the sake of all of us.'

Cork pushed his fingers through his hair, leant forward and caught Stu's eye.

'What? What are you talking about? Hate to do what?'

Stu sat up and opened the top flap of the Bergen.

'Help me get this thing out,' he muttered.

Flea and Cork reached over and pulled the mobile phone out and free of the plastic sheath, then as directed placed it in front of Stu.

Stu cracked his fingers and looked down at the device like a pianist about to begin a classic piece.

He looked up at the others.

'How long has it been since the truck drove out, do you reckon?'

The others all agreed that about two and a half, maybe three hours had passed since.

Stu nodded and looked down at the phone his face wracked with concentration.

'Right, I'm making a call to HQ, OK. You must trust me. No noise, not a sound from any of you not even a sniff. This is going to be weird.'

Flea looked at Max who in turn looked at Cork. All apart from Stu were confused.

Stu switched the device on and a weak green glow lit their faces.

With two fingers he pressed the call log button.

Up popped a list of outgoing calls made on the device.

'Great, I've got the number.'

Stu cleared his throat and pressed the call button.

The four of them heard the dialling tone clearly through the pitter-patter of raindrops falling onto their cover from the branches above.

Suddenly the dialling tone was interrupted and a stern voice cracked out.

'Victor zero, zero four, this is Moat, go ahead.'

Stu crouched forward and spoke in a whispered voice that had the others recoil and frantically search each other's faces for a clue.

A chill ran down their spines. The voice was not his, he was impersonating someone but who?'

The only one amongst them who knew was Stu.

The sharp, arrogant but hushed voice he was impersonating was Vizz's.

'Victor zero, zero four. Have located all the surviving fugitives. Repeat, have located all the surviving fugitives. Our location is…'

Stu was interrupted by Moat at HQ.

'We have your co-ordinates already, northeast within the Lintebourne Military Range, confirm. Over.'

Stu shot a glance at the others, a look of utter relief spread across his and their faces.

'Affirm. Give me instructions. Over.'

The cool HQ voice now rose an octave.

'Am assuming you're clear of the fugitives to have made this call? Confirm? Over.'

Stu whispered back.

'Affirm. I'm hidden two minutes away from the group. Over.'

HQ came back immediately with clear and precise instructions as if they had been waiting for this moment for a long time.

'Victor zero, zero four, when this call ends, I want you to return immediately to the fugitive group and call a meeting with them all and I mean all and every one of them. Not one of the group should be absent…understand?

'Now, I want you to stand in the middle of the group and start a debate, forum or whatever. This is because we want precise co-ordinates of your location. This must be achieved within ten minutes. At ten minutes precisely the group will be assembled around you. At fifteen minutes, no sooner, you and Romeo zero, zero three will then have one hour to clear the site. Understand? Over.'

Stu replied solemnly,

'Understood, sir. Over.'

HQ closed the call with.

'Ten minutes starting from, five, four, three, two, one, NOW... Moat, Hotel-Quebec out.'

There was silence apart from the sound of distant thunder, traffic and raindrops falling from the branches onto their plastic bag shelter.

Stu glanced at the others; a look of sorrow furrowed his brow.

The little group sat, damp, cold and looking at each other trying to achieve some sort of comfort in their silence.

Finally, Max reached out and placed his hand on Stu's shoulder.

'I think we all owe you a huge debt Stu. That was inspiring. Come on let's get going.'

Stu patted the mobile phone.

'Let's get the chip and battery out of this immediately. I can foresee this thing coming in useful at some point in the future.'

The black Mercedes 4x4 turned off the surfaced "B" road and threaded its way up a narrow muddy track ignoring the big red military "Warning, keep out" signs.

With low beam headlights illuminating the dense pine woodland on either side it turned off the track and wound its way through the trees up an even narrower overgrown disused track.

The driver stopped the 4x4, turned to Vizz and Rip and barked, 'Right, this is where you two get out, OK.'

Vizz reached over to the new Bergen holding the mobile phone. Pulling it across the seat he jerked back as if struck by an electric shock. He grabbed his left shoulder with his right hand. Something was vibrating … his microchip.

The second man grinned.

'Come on, come on. Cramp, is it? Not used to comfort in a smart vehicle, are you? Heh heh. Get out now, come on jump to it.'

Vizz didn't move he was as stiff as a board and convulsing. He blurted out.

'CAN'T … can't move, microchips going mad… mad in my back.'

The driver, eyes wide shot a glance to the second man and both made a panicked fumbled grab for the car door handles.

A couple of minutes earlier and two and a half kilometres to the south of the Lintebourne Range in the Partridge Hotel, Pete the caretaker had been up through the night going about his business.

This particular job saw him trying to close a window in one of the vacant upper floor rooms.

This was a small job that was number four out of seven small jobs on his list. The window had been jammed open and was letting in rainwater leaving an unsightly damp patch on the wallpaper below. As long as he kept the noise down, he shouldn't disturb the handful of sleeping guests in the other rooms.

As Pete reached up to ease the sash window free, he was blinded by an intense white mushroom of fire in the distance. The ball of light was so bright it etched into his retina as if he'd looked at the midday sun.

With eyes closed he turned away from the window and grumbled, 'What the hell! Lightning's hit somethi…'

With a crack-like thunder the blast from the explosion hit the front of the hotel like a giant spade smacking against the side of a wheelie-bin.

The top sash window frame released and dropped hitting the sill so hard every pane of glass broke. The shattered glass fell with a tinkle and crash into the car parking area below.

With the white ball still etched into his retina Pete staggered down the stairs to the girl on night reception. She looked up.

'Wow, that was close, did you hear that crash of thunder Pete?'

'Hear it? I was nearly deafened by it! It smashed the window in room eight. It wasn't me; I wasn't even near the damned window!'

Half an hour after dawn the next morning a helicopter descended through the damp low mist into a clearing in pine woodland on the Lintebourne Range.

Three personnel jumped out dressed in white biological and nuclear protection suits. They carefully adjusted each other's hoods and made straight for the site of the explosion. The last co-ordinance received showed the site at some three hundred metres southeast of their landing site.

In silence they approached. The lead figure held a Geiger counter at arm's length.

The sight that greeted their eyes was bizarre.

In the centre of an overgrown unused track, they saw what was left of a large vehicle, maybe a 4x4. The make of vehicle was just about identifiable. The bodywork had blown out and resembled a blackened, smouldering and hollow puff-fish.

In places the bodywork was almost transparent and was surrounded by a circle roughly several metres in diameter of blackened smouldering vegetation.

The nearest pine trees to the wreck showed damage, their lower branches blown away, wisps of smoke wafted upward from their charred bark.

On closer examination the three observed very little remnants of fabric, instruments or bone within the interior of wreck and only large lumps of cooling molten metal. After a thorough search around the site, they found no other debris apart from small traces of spattered molten material etched into the bark of some nearby trees.

One of the personnel taking a series of photographs of the site turned to the others and grunted, 'I'm done here.'

The other two nodded to each other and agreed, they had seen enough. Backing away they gave the site one last look then returned to the waiting helicopter.

The three carefully helped each other climb out of their protective suits and then placed them into a fridge-like metal container attached to the skid of the helicopter.

The youngest of the three climbed in, put on his headset, wiped the sweat from his brow, adjusted the microphone and commented,

'Looks to me like they could have been sheltering in an old dumped car sir.'

The man sitting beside the pilot half turned his head in reply.

'You could be right. The cleaners should be here within the hour, ha, not much for them to clean up! I'm very impressed, very impressed indeed. Absolute total destruction. You could see clearly it wasn't your usual ordinance explosion as such, no detailed debris apart from traces of molten metal. Still, must have been a huge bang though!

'The detonation of that miniscule device causes a chromosphere you see. Very impressive results, in a millisecond five times hotter than the surface of the Sun. It's the hot gases in violent motion that destroy almost all evidence. Anyway, talking of hot gasses I could do with a nice hot cup of tea when we land and I want both of your reports with those photographs on my desk by the end of today, OK?'

The third man nudged the younger and smirked.

'A brilliant field test carried out there. You could say two birds with one stone.'

Chapter Twenty

Enduring a difficult and uncomfortable trek through rain drenched undergrowth Max, Flea, Cork and Stu reached the camp two and a half days later.

They all returned exhausted, it hadn't been easy. Each had taken turns supporting Stu as he limped and stumbled along. His leg had not taken kindly to the opening of the old wound.

Flea felt a huge amount of sympathy for him.

It hadn't been that long ago that she had been lame with her injured ankle. The burden to Max had been immense. Max had not given Flea the slightest indication that he felt it was a struggle and that strengthened their relationship beyond words.

After the huge welcome Stu received from the group, especially from Nixi, they sat around a fire within the old hollow tree while Nixi gathered their sodden clothing and hung them above the fire to dry then she wrapped dry bandage around Stu's leg. Kat squeezed between Max and Cork to heat up Burdock and Sow-thistle soup which they all tucked into enthusiastically.

Later they gathered within the largest underground room in the camp, got cosy and regaled to the group about Stu's experience after becoming separated from Nixi and the incredible chance meeting at the service station.

There was split opinion on the outcome of the call to HQ made by Stu. Most agreed that the establishment would have gone ahead and pressed the button presented with the opportunity of eradicating them on mass. What would the establishment scientists have found at the site? There was no doubt that with haste they would have combed the area in detail for remains.

Could there have been any clue left to indicate to the establishment that they had not managed to achieve their goal?

From what Flea and the others had read on the destructive power of the implant device back at the establishment that fateful day, they understood that the explosion would more or less vaporise anything within several metres of the source. However, if scientists knew what they were looking for, would they be able to find it in or around the smouldering crater? A tiny scorched fragment of bone would be assumed to belong to a squirrel, fox or whatever to the unknowing eye.

Max had to re-assure the group by reminding them of the wording in one of the documents that Flea had found, "Eliminating ALL tissue and HARD Evidence". It surely meant just that.

The next morning Max, Flea and Cork did not contemplate taking a rest. Stu of course was left to rest his leg and convalesce.

The group set about improving the camouflage to the camp.

They dragged small branches to overhang the beach area, making sure that no sign of life could be spotted from above.

The escape tunnel and extra food storage rooms were attacked with vigour and planned on completion before the spring.

Simple early warning systems were built at some distance around the camp using dead ground creeper and light rotten branches. The idea was not to make the warning obvious to an approaching person or animal. A falling branch a snapping

189

twig could be heard at a fair distance but would not set alarm bells ringing by the person or people who triggered it.

All seemed happy in their work and they soon took a rest.

Begrudgingly for Max, over the following month the leadership of the group fell on his shoulders, although Cork and Flea held strong council which lifted the responsibility to some degree.

During the hours of darkness while they sheltered cosy in their underground home each evening the group planned in detail and tried to come to a decision, whether it would be in their interest or just too dangerous to move away from this camp. Should they migrate and head for a safer more secluded distant place? Would it be safer to stay put?

They all knew the risk of splitting into pairs and heading of once again on a long trek.

What would happen if they were seen and reported and one or two would definitely be spotted somewhere en route?

The establishment would suddenly swing into action realising that the fugitives had not all been killed by detonating Vizz and Rip.

The agony and danger of their big march from the establishment was still fresh in their minds.

The decision was made.

For the foreseeable future this place would be their home and their world. They would harvest their edible berries, nuts and plants near the camp so that they would not have to spend days away in risky distant places gathering them. They would try and perfect hunting and fishing, hopefully trap and bring down something small like a young Muntjac deer one day then smoke and preserve the meat for the winter months and make clothing from the skin.

The small group found immense strength in making these plans it gave them resolve to hunker down and defend this new life and freedom with a passion.

Max stood in silence on the ridge overlooking the stream and camp. He pulled his collar tighter to stop the cold rivulets of the November drizzle running down his neck and smiled.

The effectiveness of the camouflage around the camp was flawless. He nodded in pleasure. A drone or somebody hovering overhead in a helicopter looking down or in the unlikely event that someone managed to make their way through the impenetrable undergrowth would never know the camp was there.

Max realised that since his escape from the establishment, this was the first time he had truly felt secure. He straightened up and let his shoulders relax, letting out a big sigh then whispered to himself.

'Wow! They could stand right here where I'm standing now and wouldn't have a clue that a tribe of eleven strong determined, hardy little individuals lived in this spot.'

Max's thoughts turned to Ali, the only member of their group that did not survive.

'She would have loved this place.'

A soft and gentle voice replied from behind him.

'Caught you off guard Max. Naughty, naughty. What were you muttering to yourself?'

Max turned and winked at Flea.

'That was good, very stealthy. I didn't hear you approaching at all.'

Flea reached out and gently took his hand in hers.

'I guess we're all just a myth now aren't we Max? It seems weird to think that the whole world out there beyond our camp and this dense woodland hasn't a clue we exist. Well apart from the establishment and they hopefully think were dead and gone by now.'

Max nodded and squeezed her hand.

'Yes Flea, I hope so, oh and you're certainly no myth to me.'

Flea noticed a slight discomfort with Max, he had shifted from one foot to the other and looking away to her left. He seemed to be searching for something in the distance that she knew wasn't there.

'What's the matter, Max?'

Max turned, placed his arm around her shoulders and held her tight. He looked directly into her eyes and whispered softly.

'No matter what happens to us, I want to be with you for ever Flea. Is that OK?'

That big broad smile lit up Flea's face and she nodded.

'Cool.'

The End

Ingram Content Group UK Ltd.
Milton Keynes UK
UKHW021841240323
419126UK00004B/46